HINDS' FEET ON HIGH PLACES

LivingExpressionsCollection.com

This Tyndale House book by Hannah Hurnard contains the complete text of the original edition. Not one word has been omitted.

Visit Tyndale online at tyndale.com.

TYNDALE and Tyndale's quill logo are registered trademarks of Tyndale House Publishers.

Living Expressions is a trademark of Tyndale House Publishers.

Hinds' Feet on High Places: An Engaging Visual Journey

American edition text copyright © 1975 by Tyndale House Publishers. All rights reserved.

Published with the permission of The Church's Ministry among the Jews (Olive Press), London, England.

Cover and interior verse and spot illustrations copyright © Jill De Haan.

Interior illustrations copyright © Rachel McNaughton.

All images are courtesy of Freeimages.com or Unsplash.com. All rights reserved.

Designed by Jennifer L. Phelps

"Lessons Learned on the Slopes of the High Places," copyright © 1986 by Hannah Hurnard. All rights reserved.

"Hannah Hurnard: A Brief Autobiography" is adapted from *Hearing Heart*, copyright © 1975 by Tyndale House Publishers. All rights reserved.

Scripture quotations are taken or adapted from the *Holy Bible*, King James Version.

For information about special discounts for bulk purchases, please contact Tyndale House Publishers at csresponse@tyndale.com, or call 1-800-323-9400.

ISBN 978-1-4964-2467-9

Printed in China

26 25 24 23 22 21 20

13 12 11 10 9 8

CONTENTS

THE LORD GOD IS MY STRENGTH, AND HE WILL MAKE MY FEET LIKE HINDS' FEET, AND HE WILL MAKE ME TO WALK UPON MINE HIGH PLACES.

HABAKKUK 3:19

Preface to the Allegory

One morning during the daily Bible reading on our mission compound in Palestine, our little Arab nurse read from *Daily Light* a quotation from the Song of Songs, "The voice of my Beloved! behold, he cometh leaping upon the mountains, skipping upon the hills" (Song of Solomon 2:8). When asked what the verse meant, she looked up with a happy smile of understanding and said, "It means there are no obstacles which our Savior's love cannot overcome, and that to him, mountains of difficulty are as easy as an asphalt road!"

From the garden at the back of the mission house at the foot of Mount Gerizim we could often watch the gazelles bounding up the mountainside, leaping from rock to rock with extraordinary grace and agility. Their motion was one of the most beautiful examples of exultant and apparently effortless ease in surmounting obstacles which I have ever seen.

How deeply we who love the Lord of Love and desire to follow him long for the power to surmount all difficulties and tests and conflicts in life in the same exultant and triumphant way. To learn the secret of victorious living has been the heart's desire of those who love the Lord, in every generation.

We feel we would give anything if only we could, in actual experience, live on the High Places of love and victory here on this earth and during this life—able always to react to evil, tribulation, sorrow, pain, and every wrong thing in such a way that they would be overcome and transformed into something to the praise and glory of God forever. As Christians we know, in theory at least, that in the life of a child of God there are no second causes, that even the most unjust and cruel things, as well as all seemingly pointless and undeserved sufferings, have been permitted by God as a glorious opportunity for us to react to them in such a way that our Lord and Savior is able to produce in us, little by little, his own lovely character.

The Song of Songs expresses the desire implanted in every human heart, to be reunited with God himself, and to know perfect and unbroken union with him. He has made us for himself, and our hearts can never know rest and perfect satisfaction until they find it in him.

It is God's will that some of his children should learn this deep union with himself through the perfect flowering of natural human love in marriage. For others it is equally his will that the same perfect union should be learned through the experience of learning to lay down completely this natural and instinctive desire for marriage and parenthood, and accept the circumstances of life which deny them this experience. This instinct for love, so firmly implanted in the human heart, is the supreme way by which we learn to desire and love God himself above all else.

But the High Places of victory and union with Christ cannot be reached by any mental reckoning of self to be dead to sin, or by seeking to devise some way or discipline by which the will can be crucified. The only way is by learning to accept, day by day, the actual conditions and tests permitted by God, by a continually repeated laying down of our own will and acceptance of his as it is presented to us in the form of the people with whom we have to live and work, and in the things which happen to us. Every acceptance of his will becomes an altar of sacrifice, and every such surrender and abandonment of ourselves to his will is a means of furthering us on the way to the High Places to which he desires to bring every child of his while they are still living on earth.

The lessons of accepting and triumphing over evil, of becoming acquainted with grief, and pain, and, ultimately, of finding them transformed into something incomparably precious; of learning through constant glad surrender to know the Lord of Love himself in a new way and to experience unbroken union with him—these are the lessons of the allegory in this book. The High Places and the hinds' feet do not refer to heavenly places after death, but are meant to be the glorious experience of God's children here and now—if they will follow the path he chooses for them.

Perhaps the Lord will use it to speak comfort to some of his loved ones who are finding themselves forced to keep company with Sorrow and Suffering, or who walk in darkness and have no light or feel themselves tossed with tempest and not comforted. It may help them to understand a new meaning in what is happening, for the experiences through which they are passing are all part of the wonderful process by which the Lord is making real in their lives the same experience which made David and Habakkuk cry out exultantly, "The Lord God maketh my feet like hinds' feet, and setteth me upon mine High Places" (Ps. 18:33 and Hab. 3:19).

PART ONE

"Weeping may
endure
for a night"

PSALM 30:5

Invitation to the High Places

THIS IS THE STORY OF HOW Much-Afraid escaped from her Fearing relatives and went with the Shepherd to the High Places where "perfect love casteth out fear."

For several years Much-Afraid had been in the service of the Chief Shepherd, whose great flocks were pastured down in the Valley of Humiliation. She lived with her friends and fellow workers Mercy and Peace in a tranquil little white cottage in the village of Much-Trembling. She loved her work and desired intensely to please the Chief Shepherd, but happy as she was in most ways, she was conscious of several things which hindered her in her work and caused her much secret distress and shame.

In the first place she was a cripple, with feet so crooked that they often caused her to limp and stumble as she went about her work. She had also the very unsightly blemish of a crooked mouth which greatly disfigured both expression and speech and was sadly conscious that these ugly blemishes must be a cause of astonishment and offense to many who knew that she was in the service of the great Shepherd.

Most earnestly she longed to be completely delivered from these shortcomings and to be made beautiful, gracious, and strong as were so many of the Shepherd's other workers, and above all to be made like the Chief Shepherd himself. But she feared that there could be no deliverance from these two crippling disfigurements and that they must continue to mar her service always.

There was, however, another and even greater trouble in her life. She was a member of the Family of Fearings, and her relatives were scattered all over the valley, so that she could never really escape from them. An orphan, she had been brought up in the home of her aunt, poor Mrs. Dismal Forebodings, with her two cousins Gloomy and

Spiteful and their brother Craven Fear, a great bully who habitually tormented and persecuted her in a really dreadful way.

Like most of the other families who lived in the Valley of Humiliation, all the Fearings hated the Chief Shepherd and tried to boycott his servants, and naturally it was a great offense to them that one of their own family should have entered his service. Consequently they did all they could both by threats and persuasions to get her out of his employment, and one dreadful day they laid before her the family dictum that she must immediately marry her cousin Craven Fear and settle down respectably among her own people. If she refused to do this of her own free will, they threatened to use force and compel her.

Poor Much-Afraid was, of course, overwhelmed with horror at the mere idea, but her relatives always terrified her, and she had never learned to resist or ignore their threats, so she simply sat cowering before them, repeating again and again that nothing would induce her to marry Craven Fear, but she was quite unable to escape from their presence.

The unhappy interview therefore lasted a long time, and when finally they did leave her for a while, it was already early evening. With a surge of relief, Much-Afraid remembered that the Chief Shepherd would then be leading his flocks to their accustomed watering place beside a lovely cascade and pool on the outskirts of the village. To this place she was in the habit of going very early every morning to meet him and learn his wishes and commands for the day, and again in the evenings to give her report on the day's work. It was now time to meet him there beside the pool, and she felt sure he would help her and not permit her relatives to kidnap her and force her to leave his service for the dreadful slavery of marriage with Craven Fear.

Still shaking with fear and without pausing to wash the tears from her face, Much-Afraid shut the door of the cottage and started off for the cascade and the pool.

The quiet evening light was filling the Valley of Humiliation with a golden glow as she left the village and started to cross the fields. Beyond the river, the mountains which bounded the eastern side of the Valley like towering ramparts were already tinged with pink, and their deep gorges were filled with lovely and mysterious shadows.

Through the quiet and peace of this tranquil evening, poor, terrified Much-Afraid came to the pool where the Shepherd was waiting for her and told him of her dreadful plight.

"What shall I do?" she cried as she ended the recital. "How can I escape? They can't really force me to marry my cousin Craven, can they? Oh!" cried she, overwhelmed again at the very thought of such a prospect, "it is dreadful enough to be Much-Afraid, but to think of having to be Mrs. Craven Fear for the rest of my life and never able to escape from the torment of it is more than I can bear."

"Don't be afraid," said the Shepherd gently. "You are in my service, and if you will trust me they will not be able to force you against your will into any family alliance. But you ought never to have let your Fearing relatives into your cottage, because they are enemies of the King who has taken you into his employment."

"I know, oh, I know," cried Much-Afraid, "but whenever I meet any of my relatives I seem to lose all my strength and simply cannot resist them, no matter how I strive. As long as I live in the Valley I cannot escape meeting them. They are everywhere and now that they are determined to get me into their power again I shall never dare venture outside my cottage alone for fear of being kidnapped."

As she spoke she lifted her eyes and looked across the Valley and the river to the lovely sunset-lighted peaks of the mountains, then cried out in desperate longing, "Oh, if only I could escape from this Valley of Humiliation altogether and go to the High Places, completely out of reach of all the Fearings and my other relatives!"

No sooner were these words uttered when to her complete astonishment the Shepherd answered, "I have waited a long time to hear you make that suggestion, Much-Afraid. It would indeed be best for you to leave the Valley for the High Places, and I will very willingly take you there myself. The lower slopes of those mountains on the other side of the river are the borderland of my Father's Kingdom, the Realm of Love. No Fears of any kind are able to live there because 'perfect love casteth out fear and everything that torments.'"

Much-Afraid stared at him in amazement. "Go to the High Places," she exclaimed, "and live there? Oh, if only I could! For months past the longing has never left me. I think of it day and night, but it is not possible. I could never get there. I am too lame." She looked down at her malformed feet as she spoke, and her eyes again filled with tears and despair and self-pity. "These mountains are so steep and dangerous. I have been told that only the hinds and the deer can move on them safely."

"It is quite true that the way up to the High Places is both difficult and dangerous," said the Shepherd. "It has to be, so that nothing which is an enemy of Love can make the ascent and invade the Kingdom. Nothing blemished or in any way imperfect is allowed there, and the inhabitants of the High Places do need 'hinds' feet.' I have them myself," he added with a smile, "and like a young hart or a roebuck I can go leaping on the mountains and skipping on the hills with the greatest ease and pleasure.

"But, Much-Afraid, I could make yours like hinds' feet also, and set you upon the High Places. You could serve me then much more fully and be out of reach of all your enemies. I am delighted to hear that you have been longing to go there, for, as I said before, I have been waiting for you to make that suggestion. Then," he added, with another smile, "you would never have to meet Craven Fear again."

Much-Afraid stared at him in bewilderment. "Make my feet like hinds' feet," she repeated. "How is that possible? And what would the inhabitants of the Kingdom of Love say to the presence of a wretched little cripple with an ugly face and a twisted mouth, if nothing blemished and imperfect may dwell there?"

"It is true," said the Shepherd, "that you would have to be changed before you could live on the High Places, but if you are willing to go with me, I promise to help you develop hinds' feet. Up there on the mountains, as you get near the real High Places, the air is fresh and invigorating. It strengthens the whole body and there are streams with wonderful healing properties, so that those who bathe in them find all their blemishes and disfigurements washed away.

"But there is another thing I must tell you. Not only would I have to make your feet like hinds' feet, but you would have to receive another name, for it would be as impossible for a Much-Afraid to enter the Kingdom of Love as for any other member of the Fearing family. Are you willing to be changed completely, Much-Afraid, and to be made like the new name which you will receive if you become a citizen in the Kingdom of Love?"

She nodded her head and then said very earnestly, "Yes, I am."

Again he smiled, but added gravely, "There is still one thing more, the most important of all. No one is allowed to dwell in the Kingdom of Love, unless they have the flower of Love already blooming in their hearts. Has Love been planted in your heart, Much-Afraid?"

As the Shepherd said this he looked at her very steadily and she realized that his eyes were searching into the very depths of her heart and knew all that was there far better than she did herself. She did not answer for a long time, because she was not sure what to say, but she looked rather flinchingly into the eyes which were gazing at her so penetratingly and became aware that they had the power of reflecting what they looked upon.

She could thus really see her own heart as he saw it, so after a long pause she answered, "I think that what is growing there is a great longing to experience the joy of natural, human love and to learn to love supremely one person who will love me in return. But perhaps that desire, natural and right as it seems, is not the Love of which you are speaking?" She paused and then added honestly and almost tremblingly, "I see the longing to be loved and admired growing in my heart, Shepherd, but I don't think I see the kind of Love that you are talking about, at least, nothing like the love which I see in you."

"Then will you let me plant the seed of true Love there now?" asked the Shepherd. "It will take you some time to develop hinds' feet and to climb to the High Places, and if I put the seed in your heart now it will be ready to bloom by the time you get there."

Much-Afraid shrank back. "I am afraid," she said. "I have been told that if you really love someone you give that loved one the power to hurt and pain you in a way nothing else can."

"That is true," agreed the Shepherd. "To love does mean to put yourself into the power of the loved one and to become very vulnerable to pain, and you are very Much-Afraid of pain, are you not?"

She nodded miserably and then said shamefacedly, "Yes, very much afraid of it."

"But it is so happy to love," said the Shepherd quietly. "It is happy to love even if you are not loved in return. There is pain too, certainly, but Love does not think that very significant."

Much-Afraid thought suddenly that he had the most patient eyes she had ever seen. At the same time there was something in them that hurt her to the heart, though she could not have said why, but she still shrank back in fear and said (bringing the words out very quickly because somehow she was ashamed to say them), "I would never dare to love unless I were sure of being loved in return. If

I let you plant the seed of Love in my heart will you give me the promise that I shall be loved in return? I couldn't bear it otherwise."

The smile he turned on her then was the gentlest and kindest she had ever seen, yet once again, and for the same indefinable reason as before, it cut her to the quick. "Yes," he said, without hesitation, "I promise you, Much-Afraid, that when the plant of Love is ready to bloom in your heart and when you are ready to change your name, then you will be loved in return."

A thrill of joy went through her from head to foot. It seemed too wonderful to be believed, but the Shepherd himself was making the promise, and of one thing she was quite sure. He could not lie. "Please plant Love in my heart now," she said faintly. Poor little soul, she was still Much-Afraid even when promised the greatest thing in the world.

The Shepherd put his hand in his bosom, drew something forth, and laid it in the palm of his hand. Then he held his hand out toward Much-Afraid. "Here is the seed of Love," he said.

She bent forward to look, then gave a startled little cry and drew back. There was indeed a seed lying in the palm of his hand, but it was shaped exactly like a long, sharply-pointed thorn. Much-Afraid had often noticed that the Shepherd's hands were scarred and wounded, but now she saw that the scar in the palm of the hand held out to her was the exact shape and size of the seed of Love lying beside it.

"The seed looks very sharp," she said shrinkingly. "Won't it hurt if you put it into my heart?"

He answered gently, "It is so sharp that it slips in very quickly. But, Much-Afraid, I have already warned you that Love and Pain go together, for a time at least. If you would know Love, you must know pain too."

Much-Afraid looked at the thorn and shrank from it. Then she looked at the Shepherd's face and repeated his words to herself. "When the seed of Love in your heart is ready to bloom, you will be loved in return," and a strange new courage entered into her. She suddenly stepped forward, bared her heart, and said, "Please plant the seed here in my heart."

His face lit up with a glad smile and he said with a note of joy in his voice, "Now you will be able to go with me to the High Places and be a citizen in the Kingdom of my Father."

Then he pressed the thorn into her heart. It was true, just as he had said, it did cause a piercing pain, but it slipped in quickly and then, suddenly, a sweetness she had never felt or imagined before tingled through her. It was bittersweet, but the sweetness was the stronger. She thought of the Shepherd's words, "It is so happy to love," and her pale, sallow cheeks suddenly glowed pink and her eyes shone. For a moment Much-Afraid did not look afraid at all. The twisted mouth had relaxed into a happy curve, and the shining eyes and pink cheeks made her almost beautiful.

"Thank you, thank you," she cried, and knelt at the Shepherd's feet. "How good you are. How patient you are.

There is no one in the whole world as good and kind as you. I will go with you to the mountains. I will trust you to make my feet like hinds' feet, and to set me, even me, upon the High Places."

"I am more glad even than you," said the Shepherd, "and now you really act as though you are going to change your name already. But there is one thing more I must tell you. I shall take you to the foot of the mountains myself, so that there will be no danger from your enemies. After that, two special companions I have chosen will guide and help you on all the steep and difficult places while your feet are still lame and while you can only limp and go slowly.

"You will not see me all the time, Much-Afraid, for as I told you, I shall be leaping on the mountains and skipping on the hills, and you will not at first be able to accompany me or keep up with me. That will come later. However, you must remember that as soon as you reach the slopes of the mountains there is a wonderful system of communication from end to end of the Kingdom of Love, and I shall be able to hear you whenever you speak to me. Whenever you call for help I promise to come to you at once.

"At the foot of the mountains my two servants whom I have chosen to be your guides will be waiting for you. Remember, I have chosen them myself, with great care, as the two who are most able to help you and

assist you in developing hinds' feet. You will accept them with joy and allow them to be your helpers, will you not?"

"Oh, yes," she answered at once, smiling at him happily. "Of course I am quite certain that you know best and that whatever you choose is right." Then she added joyfully, "I feel as though I shall never be afraid again."

He looked very kindly at the little shepherdess who had just received the seed of Love into her heart and was preparing to go with him to the High Places, but also with full understanding. He knew her through and through, in all the intricate labyrinth of her lonely heart, better far than she knew herself. No one understood better than he, that growing into the likeness of a new name is a long process, but he did not say this. He looked with a certain tender pity and compassion at the glowing cheeks and shining eyes which had so suddenly transformed the appearance of plain little Much-Afraid.

Then he said, "Now you may go home and make your preparations for leaving. You are not to take anything with you, only leave everything in order. Do not tell anyone about it, for a journey to the High Places needs to be a secret matter. I cannot now give you the exact time when we are to start for the mountains, but it will be soon, and you must be ready to follow me whenever I come to the cottage and call. I will give you a secret sign. I shall sing one of the Shepherd's songs as I pass the cottage, and it will contain a special message for you. When you hear it, come at once and follow me to the trysting place."

Then, as the sun had already gone down in a blaze of red and gold, and the eastern mountains were now veiled in misty mauve and grey, and the shadows were lengthening, he turned and led his flock away toward the sheepfolds.

Much-Afraid turned her face homeward, her heart full of happiness and excitement, and still feeling as though she would never be frightened again. As she started back across the fields she sang to herself one of the songs from an old book of songs which the shepherds often used. Never before had it seemed to her so sweet, so applicable.

"The song of Songs," the loveliest song,
The song of Love the King,
No joy on earth compares with his,
But seems a broken thing.
His Name as ointment is poured forth,
And all his lovers sing.
Draw me—I will run after thee,
Thou art my heart's one choice,
Oh, bring me to thy royal house,
To dwell there and rejoice.
There in thy presence, O my King,
To feast and hear thy voice.
Look not upon me with contempt,
Though soiled and marred I be,
The King found me—an outcast thing—
And set his love on me.
I shall be perfected by Love,
Made fair as day to see.

CANT. 1:1-6

She walked singing across the first field and was halfway over the next when suddenly she saw Craven Fear himself coming toward her. Poor Much-Afraid; for a little while she had completely forgotten the existence of her dreadful relatives, and now here was the most dreaded and detested of them all slouching toward her. Her heart filled with a terrible panic. She looked right and left, but there was no hiding place anywhere, and besides it was all too obvious that he was actually coming to meet her, for as soon as he saw her he quickened his pace and in a moment or two was right beside her.

With a horror that sickened her very heart she heard him say, "Well, here you are at last, little Cousin Much-Afraid. So we are to be married, eh, what do you think of that?" and he pinched her, presumably in a playful manner, but viciously enough to make her gasp and bite her lips to keep back a cry of pain.

She shrank away from him and shook with terror and loathing. Unfortunately this was the worst thing she could have done, for it was always her obvious fear which encouraged him to continue tormenting her. If only she could have ignored him, he soon would have tired of teasing and of her company and would have wandered off to look for other prey. In all her life, however, Much-Afraid had never been able to ignore Fear. Now it was absolutely beyond her power to conceal the dread which she felt.

Her white face and terrified eyes immediately had the effect of stimulating Craven's desire to bait her. Here she was, alone and completely in his power. He caught hold of her, and poor Much-Afraid uttered one frenzied cry of terror and pain. At that moment Craven Fear loosed his grasp and cringed away.

The Shepherd had approached them unperceived and was standing beside them. One look at his stern face and flashing eyes and the stout Shepherd's cudgel grasped in his strong, uplifted hand was more than enough for the bully. Craven Fear slunk away like a whipped cur, actually running from the village instead of toward it, not knowing where he was going, urged by one instinct alone, to find a place of safety.

Much-Afraid burst into tears. Of course she ought to have known that Craven was a coward and that if only she had lifted her voice and called for the Shepherd, he would have fled at once. Now her dress was torn and disordered, and her arms bruised by the bully's grip, yet that was the least part of her distress. She was overwhelmed with shame that she had so quickly acted like her old name and nature, which she had hoped was beginning to be changed already.

It seemed so impossible to ignore the Fearings, still less to resist them. She did not dare look at the Shepherd, but had she done so she would have seen with what compassion he was regarding her. She did not realize that the Prince of Love is "of very tender compassions to them that are afraid." She supposed that, like everybody else, he was despising her for her silly fears, so she muttered a shamed "thank you."

Then, still without looking at him, she limped painfully toward the village, weeping bitterly as she went and saying over and over again to herself, "What is the use of even thinking of going to the High Places? I could never reach them, for the least little thing is enough to turn me back."

However, when at last she reached the security of the cottage she began to feel better, and by the time she had drunk a cup of tea and taken her evening meal she had recovered so far that she was able to remind herself of all that had happened there beside the cascade and the pool. Suddenly she remembered, with a thrill of wonder and delight, that the seed of Love had been planted in her heart. As she thought of it, the same almost intolerable sweetness stole over her, the bittersweet, indefinable but wholly delightful ecstasy of a new happiness.

"It is happy to love," said little Much-Afraid to herself and then she repeated: "It is happy to love." After putting the cottage in order for the night, because she was utterly tired out with all the conflicting emotions of that strange day, she went to bed. Lying there before falling asleep, she sang over and over again to herself another of the lovely songs from the old song book.

O thou whom my soul loveth,
Tell me where thou dost feed,
And where thy flocks at noonday
To rest and browse dost lead.
For why should I
By other be,
And not by thee?
O fairest among women,
Dost thou indeed not know?
Then lead my little flocklet
The way that my flocks go;
And be to me,
As I to thee
Sweet company.

CANT. 1:7-8

Then she fell into a heavy, dreamless sleep.

2

Fearing Invasion

Much-Afraid woke early the next morning and all her fears were gone. Her first thought was, "Probably sometime today I am to start for the High Places with the Shepherd." This so excited her that she could hardly eat her breakfast, and as she began making arrangements for her departure, she could not help singing.

It seemed to her that ever since the seed of Love had been planted in her heart, songs of joy were welling up in her innermost being. And the songs which best expressed this new happiness and thankfulness were from the old book which the shepherds so loved to use as they worked among the flocks and led them to the pastures. As she carried out the simple arrangements the Shepherd had told her to make, she sang another of these songs.

Now when the King at table sits,
My spikenard smelleth sweet,
And myrrh and camphire from my store
I pour upon his feet.

My thankful love must be displayed,
He loved and wooed a beggar maid.
Ye daughters of Jerusalem,
I'm black to look upon
As goatskin tents; but also as
The tent of Solomon.
Without, I bear the marks of sin,
But Love's adorning is within.
Despise me not that I am black,
The sun hath burned my face,
My mother's children hated me,
And drove me from my place.
In their vineyards I toiled and wept.
But mine own vineyard have not kept.
I am not fair save to the King,
Though fair my royal dress,
His kingly grace is lavished on
My need and worthlessness.
My blemishes he will not see
But loves the beauty that shall be.

CANT. 1:12-15, 5-6

From time to time as she went about her work her heart fluttered, half with excitement, half with dread of the unknown, but whenever she remembered the thorn in her heart, she tingled from head to foot with the same mysterious sweetness. Love was for her, too, even for her, crippled little Much-Afraid. When she reached the High Places she was to lose her humiliating disfigurements and be made beautiful, and when the plant in her heart was ready to bloom she was to be loved in return. Even as she thought of this, doubt mingled with the sweetness. Surely it could not possibly be true; just a beautiful dream, but not reality.

"Oh, I am afraid it won't ever happen," she would say to herself, and then, when she thought of the Shepherd, her heart quickened again and she would run to the door or window to see if he were coming to call her.

The morning wore on and still he had not come, but just after midday something else came: an invasion by her terrible relatives. All of a sudden, before she realized what was happening, they were upon her. There was tramping of feet and a clamor of voices and then she was surrounded by a whole army of aunts and uncles and cousins. Craven, however, was not with them. The family, hearing of his reception the evening before, and realizing that she shrank

from him with peculiar dread and terror, had decided that it would not be wise to take him with them.

They were determined to overrule Much-Afraid's objections to the marriage, and if possible get her out of the cottage and into one of their own dwelling places. Their plan was to make a bold attack while she would be alone in the cottage and the Shepherd far away with his flocks, so they hoped she would be at their mercy. She could not be forcibly abducted in broad daylight; there were too many of the Shepherd's servants in the village who would instantly come to her assistance.

However, they knew Much-Afraid's timidity and weakness and they believed that, if there were enough of them present, they could cow her into consenting to go with them to the Mansion of old Lord Fearing. Then they would have her in their power.

The old Lord himself was actually with them, assuring her in a fatherly tone of voice that they had come with the kindest and friendliest intentions. He understood that she had some objections to the proposed marriage, and he wanted to have the opportunity of quietly talking them over with her, to see if he could set them at rest. It seemed to him that it was a suitable and attractive match in every way and that there must be some extraordinary misconception in her mind which a little understanding talk together would set right. If not, he assured her kindly, he would not permit her to be married against her will.

When he had finished, a babel of other Fearing voices broke in, reasoning with her and making all sorts of suggestions. The fact was, they told her, that she had cut herself off from her relatives for so long, it was now quite apparent that she had all kinds of strange notions about their feelings and intentions toward her. It was really only right that she should now spend a little time with them and thus give them the opportunity of proving that she had misjudged and misunderstood them.

Craven might not be just as handsome and pleasing in appearance as a prince in a fairy tale, and it was true that he had, unfortunately, rather a rough manner, but that was because he had known nothing of the softening and refining influences of marriage. Certainly the responsibilities and joys of married life would quickly alter this, and would indeed effect a transformation in him. It was to be her delightful privilege to assist as principal mover in bringing about this reformation which they all so eagerly wished to see.

The whole gang talked on and on, while poor Much-Afraid sat cowering in their midst, almost too dazed to know what they were saying and suggesting. Just as they had hoped, they were gradually bringing her to a state of bewilderment and incoherent fear. It looked as though they would soon be able to persuade her that it was her duty to attempt the impossible task of trying to convert Craven Fear into something less objectionable than he really was. Suddenly there came an interruption from without.

The Fearings had carefully closed the door when they entered the cottage and even contrived to bolt it, so that Much-Afraid could not escape. Now came the distant sound of a man's voice raised in song, singing one of the songs from the old book which Much-Afraid knew and loved so well. Then the singer himself came in view, slowly passing along the lane. It was the Chief Shepherd, already leading his flock to the watering place. The words floated in through the open window, accompanied by the soft bleating of the sheep and the scuffling of many little dusty feet as they pattered after him.

It seemed as though all other sounds were hushed to stillness on that quiet summer afternoon as the Shepherd sang while passing the cottage. Inside, the clamor of voices had ceased instantly and was succeeded by silence which could be felt. This is what he sang:

The Voice of my Beloved!
Through all my heart it thrills,
He leaps upon the mountains,
And skips upon the hills.
For like a roe or young hart,
So swift and strong is he,
He looketh through my window
And beckoneth unto me.
"Rise up, my love, my fair one,
And come away with me,
Gone are the snows of winter,
The rains no more we see.
The flowers are appearing,
The little birds all sing,
The turtle dove is calling,
Through all the land 'tis spring.
The shoots are on the grapevines,
The figs are on the tree,
Arise, my love, my fair one,
And come away with me.
Why is my dove still hiding?
When all things else rejoice,
Oh, let me see thee, fair one,
Oh, let me hear thy voice."

CANT. 2:8-14

What fear keeps you from moving forward when God asks?
How can you overcome this fear with the Lord's help?

Making another move in these fragile states, afraid
of it all falling apart & being left amidst the
lonely, broken ruins. Taking one step forward,
which is hard enough, and 10 steps back
→ I need deeper trust

As she sat listening in the cottage, Much-Afraid knew with a pang of agonizing pain that the Shepherd was calling her to go with him to the mountains. This was the secret signal he had promised, and he had said that she must be ready to leave instantly, the moment she heard it. Now here she was, locked inside her own cottage, beleaguered by her terrible Fears and unable to respond in any way to his call or even to give any sign of her need.

There was one moment indeed, when the song first started and everyone was startled into silence, when she might have called to him to come and help her. She did not realize that the Fearings were holding their breath lest she did call, and had she done so, they would have fled helter-skelter through the door. However, she was too stunned with fear to seize the opportunity, and then it was too late.

The next moment she felt Coward's heavy hand laid tightly over her mouth, then other hands gripped her firmly and held her in the chair. So the Shepherd slowly passed the cottage, "showing himself at the window," and singing the signal song, but receiving no response of any kind.

When he had passed and the words of the song and the bleating of the sheep had died away in the distance, it was found that Much-Afraid had fainted. Her cousin Coward's gagging hands had half-choked her. Her relatives would dearly have liked to seize this opportunity and carry her off while she was unconscious, but as this was the hour when everybody was returning from work it was too dangerous. The Fearings decided therefore that they would remain in the cottage until darkness fell, then gag Much-Afraid and carry her off unperceived.

When this plan had been decided upon, they laid her upon the bed to recover as best she might, while some of the aunts and cousins went out into the kitchen to see what provisions for refreshing themselves might be plundered. The men sat smoking in the sitting room, and Gloomy was left to guard the half-conscious victim in the bedroom.

Gradually Much-Afraid regained her senses, and as she realized her position she nearly fainted again with horror. She dared not cry out for help, for all her neighbors would be away at their work; but were they? No, it was later than she had thought, for suddenly she heard the voice of Mrs. Valiant, her neighbor in the cottage next door. At the sound, Much-Afraid braced herself for one last desperate bid for escape.

Gloomy was quite unprepared for such a move, and before she realized what was happening, Much-Afraid sprang from the bed and shouted through the window as loudly as her fear permitted, "Valiant! Valiant! Come and help me. Come quickly. Help!"

At the sound of her first cry, Mrs. Valiant looked across the garden and caught a glimpse of Much-Afraid's white, terrified face at the window and of her hand beckoning entreatingly. The next moment the face was jerked away from view and a curtain suddenly drawn across the window. That was enough for Mrs. Valiant, whose name described her exactly. She hurried straight across to her neighbor's cottage and tried the door, but finding it locked, she looked in through a window and saw the room full of Much-Afraid's relatives.

Mrs. Valiant was not the sort of person to be the least intimidated by what she called, "a pack of idle Fears." Thrusting her face right in through the window, she cried in a threatening voice.

"Out of this house you go, this minute, every one of you. If you have not left in three seconds, I shall call the Chief Shepherd. This cottage belongs to him, and won't you catch it if he finds you here."

The effect of her words was magical. The door was unbolted and thrown open and the Fearings poured out pell-mell, tumbling over one another in their haste to get away. Mrs. Valiant smiled grimly as she watched their ignominious flight. When the last one had scuttled away she went into the cottage to Much-Afraid, who seemed quite overcome with fear and distress. Little by little she learned the story of those hours of torment and the plan to kidnap the poor victim after darkness fell.

Mrs. Valiant hardly knew herself what it was to feel fear, and had just routed the whole gang of Fearings singlehanded. She felt much inclined to adopt a bracing attitude and to chide the silly girl for not standing up to her relatives at once, boldly repulsing them before they got her into their clutches. But as she looked at the white face and terrified eyes and saw the quaking body of poor Much-Afraid, she checked herself. "What is the use of saying it? She can't act upon it, poor thing; she is one of them herself and has got Fearing in the blood, and when the enemy is within you it's a poor prospect. I think no one but the Shepherd himself can really help her," she reflected.

So instead of an admonition, she patted the trembling girl and said with all the kindness of her motherly heart, "Now, my dear, while you are getting over your fright, I'll just pop into the kitchen and make a good cup of tea for both of us and you'll feel better at once. My! If they haven't been in here and put the kettle on for us," she added, as she opened the kitchen door and found the cloth already on the table and the preparations for the plundered meal which the unwanted visitors had so hastily abandoned.

"What a pack of harpies," she muttered angrily to herself, then smiled complacently as she remembered how they had fled before her.

By the time they had drunk their tea and Mrs. Valiant had energetically cleared away the last traces of the unwelcome invaders, Much-Afraid had nearly recovered her composure. Darkness had long since fallen, and now it was much too late for her to go to the pool to keep tryst with the Shepherd and explain why she had not responded to his call. She would have to wait for the morning light. So at Mrs. Valiant's suggestion, as she was feeling utterly exhausted, she went straight to bed. Her neighbor saw her safely tucked in, and kissed her warmly and reassuringly. Indeed, she offered to sleep in the cottage herself that night, but Much-Afraid, knowing that she had a family waiting for her at home, refused the kind offer. However, before leaving, Mrs. Valiant placed a bell beside her bed and assured her that if anything alarmed her in the night she had only to ring the bell and the whole Valiant family would be over instantly to assist her. Then she went away and Much-Afraid was left alone in the cottage.

Flight in the Night

FOR HOURS POOR MUCH-AFRAID lay sleepless on her bed, too bruised in mind and body to rest in one position, but tossing and turning wearily from side to side until long after midnight. Somewhere at the back of her mind was a dreadful uneasiness, as though there was something she ought to remember, but was unable to do so. When at last she fell asleep this thought still haunted her.

She woke suddenly an hour or two later, her mind intensely alert, conscious of an agonizing pain such as she had never known before. The thorn in her heart was throbbing and aching in a manner she could scarcely bear. It was as though the pain was hammering out something which at first she was still too confused to be able to understand. Then, all of a sudden, in a terrible flash, it became clear to her, and she found herself whispering over and over again, "The Shepherd came and called me as he promised, but I didn't go to him or give any answer.

Supposing he thought that I had changed my mind and didn't want to go with him. Supposing he has gone and left me behind! Gone without me! Yes, left me behind!"

The shock of this thought was awful. This was the thing she had forgotten. He would not be able to understand why she had not gone out to him as he had told her.

He had urged her to be ready to go with him the instant that he called, that there must be no delay, that he himself had to go to the mountains on urgent business. She had not been able to go even to the trysting place as usual that evening.

Of course he would think that she was afraid. Perhaps he was gone already and alone. Much-Afraid turned icy cold and her teeth chattered, but it was the pain in her heart which was the most awful part of her distress. It seemed to suffocate her as she lay there in bed. She sat up, shivering with cold and with the horror of the thought. She could not bear it if he had gone and left her behind.

On the table beside her lay the old song book. Glancing down at it in the light of the lamp, she saw it was open at the page whereon was written a song about another shepherdess. She, just like herself, had failed to respond to the call of Love and then found, too late, that Love had gone away.

It had always seemed to her such a sad song that she could hardly read it, but now as she read the words again in the dark loneliness of the night, it seemed as though it was the cry of her own forlorn and terrified heart.

By night on my bed I sought him,
He whom my soul loveth so.
I sought—but I could not find him,
And now I will rise and go—
Out in the streets of the city,
And out on the broad highway;
For he whom my soul so loveth,
Hath left me and gone away.

The page in the little song book ended there, and she did not turn the leaf. Suddenly she could bear the uncertainty no longer. She must see for herself at once if he really had gone away and left her behind. She slipped out of bed, dressed herself as quickly as her shaking fingers would permit, and then unlocked the cottage door. She, too, would go out into the street and the broad highway and would see if she could find him, would see if he had gone and left her behind, or—oh, if only it were possible—if he had waited to give her another chance.

Opening the door, she went out into the darkness. A hundred Craven Fears lurking in the lonely street could not have deterred her at that moment, for the pain in her heart swallowed up fear and everything else and drove her

forth. So in the dark hours, just before the dawn, Much-Afraid started off to look for the Shepherd.

She could not go quickly because of her lameness, but limped along the village streets toward the open fields and the sheepfolds. As she went she whispered to herself, "O Shepherd, when you said that Love and pain go together, how truly you spoke."

Had she but known or even dimly sensed what it would be like, would she, could she, possibly have consented to let him put the thorn in her heart? It was too late now: it was there. Love was there and pain, too, and she must find the Shepherd. At last, limping and breathless, she came to the sheepfolds, still and silent in the dim starlight. One or two undershepherds were there, keeping watch over the flocks through the night, and when they heard footsteps approaching they rose up from the ground and went to meet the intruder.

"Who are you?" they challenged her in the darkness, then stared in amazement as their lanterns flashed on the white face and frightened eyes of Much-Afraid.

"Is the Chief Shepherd here?" she gasped as she leaned against the wall of the sheepfold, panting and trying to recover her breath.

"No," said the watchman, staring at her curiously. "He left the flocks in our charge this night and gave his orders. He said that he had to make a journey to the mountains, as he often does, and did not say when he would be back."

Much-Afraid could not speak. She moaned and pressed her hands to her heart, feeling as though it would break. What could she do now? He was gone. He had thought that she did not want to go and had not waited for her. Then, aching with despair, as she leaned tremblingly against the wall of the fold, she remembered the Shepherd's face and the loving-kindness of the look with which he had invited her to accompany him to the mountains.

It came to her mind that he who understood her so well, who knew all about her fears and had compassion on her, would not leave until he was quite sure that she really meant to refuse to go with him. She lifted her eyes, looked across the Valley toward the eastern mountains and the High Places. A faint streak of light was appearing in the east, and she knew that soon the sun would rise. Suddenly she remembered the last verse of the sad song which she had read, the last verse on the page which she had not waited to turn over. It came whispering into her mind just as a little bird began to sing in one of the bushes beside her.

And then—in the dawn I saw him.
He whom my heart loveth so.
I found him, held him and told him
I never could let him go.

CANT. 3:1-5

Much-Afraid ceased trembling and said to herself, "I will go to the trysting-place, and see if he is waiting for me there." With scarcely a word to the watchmen she turned and hurried southward, over the field where Craven Fear had met her toward the sheep pool. Almost forgetting that she was lame, she sped toward the distant trees which fringed the pool.

Just as the sky turned red above the mountains, the joyous, babbling sound of cascading water reached her ears, and as she hurried forward Much-Afraid suddenly found a cascade of song pouring forth from her own heart.

He was there, standing by the pool, looking toward her with the light of the sunrise shining on his face. As Much-Afraid stumbled toward him, he stepped quickly to her side and she fell at his feet sobbing, "O my Lord, take me with you as you said. Don't leave me behind."

"I knew you would come," he said gently, "but Much-Afraid, why were you not at the trysting-place last evening? Did you not hear me when I passed your cottage and called? I wanted to tell you to be ready to start with me this morning at sunrise." As he spoke the sun rose fully over the peaks of the mountains and bathed them both in a lovely golden light.

"I am here," said Much-Afraid, still kneeling at his feet, "and I will go with you anywhere."

Then the Shepherd took her by the hand and they started for the mountains.

4

Start for the High Places

IT WAS EARLY MORNING of a beautiful day. The valley lay as though still asleep. The only sounds were the joyful laughter of the running streams and the gay little songs of the birds. The dew sparkled on the grass and the wild flowers glowered like little jewels. Especially lovely were the wild anemones, purple, pink and scarlet, which dotted the pastures everywhere, thrusting their beautiful little faces up through the straggling thorns. Sometimes the Shepherd and Much-Afraid walked over patches of thousands of tiny little pink or mauve blossoms, each minutely small and yet all together forming a brilliant carpet, far richer than any seen in a king's palace.

Once the Shepherd stooped and touched the flowers gently with his fingers, then said to Much-Afraid with a smile, "Humble yourself, and you will find that Love is spreading a carpet of flowers beneath your feet."

Much-Afraid looked at him earnestly. "I have often wondered about the wild flowers," she said. "It does seem strange that such unnumbered multitudes should bloom in the wild places of the earth where perhaps nobody ever sees them and the goats and the cattle can walk over them and crush them to death. They have so much beauty and sweetness to give and no one on whom to lavish it, nor who will even appreciate it."

The look the Shepherd turned on her was very beautiful. "Nothing my Father and I have made is ever wasted," he said quietly, "and the little wild flowers have a wonderful lesson to teach. They offer themselves so sweetly and confidently and willingly, even if it seems that there is no one to appreciate them. Just as though they sang a joyous little song to themselves, that it is so happy to love, even though one is not loved in return.

"I must tell you a great truth, Much-Afraid, which only the few understand. All the fairest beauties in the human soul, its greatest victories, and its most splendid achievements are always those which no one else knows anything about, or can only dimly guess at. Every inner response of the human heart to Love and every conquest over self-love is a new flower on the tree of Love.

"Many a quiet, ordinary, and hidden life, unknown to the world, is a veritable garden in which Love's flowers and fruits have come to such perfection that it is a place of delight where the King of Love himself walks and rejoices with his friends. Some of my servants have indeed won great visible victories and are rightly loved and reverenced by other men, but always their greatest victories are like the wild flowers, those which no one knows about. Learn this lesson now, down here in the valley, Much-Afraid, and when you get to the steep places of the mountains it will comfort you."

Then he added, "Come, the birds are all singing so joyously, let us join them too, and the flowers shall suggest the theme of our song." So, as they walked down the Valley toward the river, they sang together another of the old songs in the Shepherd's book, singing the parts in turn.

I am the Rose of Sharon,
A wild anemone.
As lily 'mong the thorn trees
So is my love to me.
An apple tree 'mong wild trees,
My Love is in my sight,
I sit down in his shadow,
His fruit is my delight.
He brought me to his palace,
And to the banquet hall,
To share with me his greatness,
I, who am least of all.
Oh, give me help and comfort,
For I am sick with shame,
Unfit to be his consort,
Unfit to bear his Name.
I charge you, o ye daughters,
Ye roes among the trees,
Stir not my sleeping loved one,
To love me e'er he please.

CANT. 2:1-4, 7

Just as they finished singing this song they came to a place where a rushing stream poured itself across the path they were following and went cascading down the other side. It was running so swiftly and singing so loudly that it seemed to fill the valley around them with its laughing voice.

As the Shepherd lifted Much-Afraid across the slippery, wet stones she said to him, "I do wish I knew what it is that all running water sings.

"Sometimes in the silence of the night I lie in bed and listen to the voice of the little stream which runs past our cottage garden. It sounds so happy and so eager, and as though it were repeating to itself over and over again some very lovely, secret message. I think all running water seems to be singing the same song, either loud and clear or soft and low. I do wish I knew what the waters were saying. It is quite different from the voice of the sea and of salt waters, but I never can understand it. It is an unknown tongue. Tell me, Shepherd, do you know what all the waters sing as they hurry on their way?"

The Shepherd smiled again, and they stood silently for a few moments by the little torrent, which seemed to shout even more loudly and exultantly as though it knew they had paused to listen. Suddenly, as Much-Afraid stood beside the Shepherd it seemed as though her ears and her understanding were open, and bit by bit, the water-language became clear. It is, of course, impossible to write it in water-language, but this is the best I can do to translate it. Of course, it is a very poor effort, for though a water song perhaps may be set to music, words are quite a different matter. But it went something like this:

THE WATER SONG

Come, oh come! let us away—
Lower, lower every day,
Oh, what joy it is to race
Down to find the lowest place.
This the dearest law we know—
"It is happy to go low."
Sweetest urge and sweetest will,
"Let us go down lower still."
Hear the summons night and day
Calling us to come away.
From the heights we leap and flow
To the valleys down below.
Always answering to the call,
To the lowest place of all.
Sweetest urge and sweetest pain,
To go low and rise again.

"That is very puzzling," said Much-Afraid, after she had listened for a little and found that this was the refrain, repeated over and over again, though with a thousand variations of little trills and murmurs and bubbles and splashing sighs.

"'Let us go down lower still,' the water seems to be singing so gladly, because it is hurrying to go down to the lowest place, and yet you are calling me to the Highest Places. What does it mean?"

"The High Places," answered the Shepherd, "are the starting places for the journey down to the lowest place in the world. When you have hinds' feet and can go 'leaping on the mountains and skipping on the hills,' you will be able, as I am, to run down from the heights in gladdest self-giving and then go up to the mountains again. You will be able to mount to the High Places swifter than eagles, for it is only up on the High Places of Love that anyone can receive the power to pour themselves down in an utter abandonment of self-giving."

This saying seemed very mysterious and strange, but now that her ears had been opened to understand the water song, she heard it repeated over and over again by all the little streams which crossed their pathway or ran beside it. It seemed, too, that the wild flowers were also singing the same sort of song, only in yet another language, a color language, which, like the water tongue, could only be understood by the heart and not by the mind. They seemed to have a little chorus all their own which thousands upon thousands of them were singing in different color notes.

> ♫ *This is the law by which we live—*
> ♪♩ *It is so sweet to give and give.*

After that it seemed to Much-Afraid that all the little birds were chirping and trilling and lilting a tiny theme song also, with unnumbered variations, but still with one chorus breaking in all the time.

> ♪ ♩ *This is the joy of all winged life above—*
> *Happy it is to be able to love.*

"I never knew before," said Much-Afraid suddenly, "that the Valley is such a beautiful place and so full of song."

The Shepherd laughed and answered, "Only Love can really understand the music and the beauty and the joy which was planted in the heart of all created things. Have you forgotten that two days ago I planted the seed of Love in your heart? Already it has begun to make you hear and see things which you did not notice before.

"As Love grows in you, Much-Afraid, you will come to understand many things which you never dreamed of before. You will develop the gift of understanding many 'unknown tongues' and you will learn to speak Love's own language too, but first you must learn to spell out the alphabet of Love and to develop hinds' feet. Both these things you will learn on the journey to the High Places, and now here we are at the river, and over on the other side the foothills of the mountains begin. There we shall find your two guides waiting for you."

It was strange and wonderful indeed, thought Much-Afraid, that they had reached the river so quickly and were already approaching the mountains. Upheld by the Shepherd's hand and supported by his strength, she had really forgotten her lameness and had been unconscious of either tiredness or weakness. Oh, if only he would take her the whole way to the mountain places, instead of giving her over to the care of other guides.

When she thought of this, she said to him imploringly, "Will you not take me all the way? When I am with you I am strong and I am sure no one else but you can get me up to the High Places."

He looked at her most kindly, but answered quietly, "Much-Afraid, I could do what you wish. I could carry you all the way up to the High Places myself, instead of leaving you to climb there. But if I did, you would never be able to develop hinds' feet, and become my companion and go where I go. If you will climb to the heights this once with the companions I have chosen for you, even though it may seem a very long and in some places a very difficult journey, I promise you that you will develop hinds' feet.

"Afterwards you will be able to go with me, 'leaping on the mountains,' and be able to make the ascent and the descent in the twinkling of an eye. Moreover, if I carry you up to the High Places now, with only a tiny seed of Love in your heart, you will not be able to live in the Kingdom of Love. You will have to stay outside on places not so high, still within reach of your enemies.

"Some of them, you know, can visit the lower parts of the mountain. I have no doubt that you will meet them as you make the ascent. That is why I have most carefully chosen for you two of the very best and strongest guides. I assure you, however, that never for a moment shall I be beyond your reach or call for help, even when you cannot see me. It is just as though I shall be present with you all the time, even though invisible. And you have my faithful promise that this journey which you are now to make will be the means of developing your hinds' feet."

"You will give me a new name when I get to the top?" quavered poor Much-Afraid, who all of a sudden seemed to have become deaf to the music around her and to be full of fears and forebodings again.

"Yes, certainly. When the flower of Love is ready to bloom in your heart, you will be loved in return and will receive a new name," replied the Shepherd.

Much-Afraid paused on the bridge and looked back over the way they had come. The Valley looked very green and peaceful, while the mountains to whose foot they had come towered above them like gigantic and threatening ramparts. Far away in the distance she could see the trees growing around the village of Much-Trembling, and with a sudden pang she pictured the Shepherd's helpers going about their happy work, the flocks wandering over the pastures and the peaceful little white cottage in which she had lived.

As these scenes rose before her, tears began to prick in her eyes and the thorn pricked in her heart, but almost at once she turned to the Shepherd and said thankfully, "I will trust you and do whatever you want."

Then, as she looked up in his face, he smiled most sweetly and said something he had never said before, "You have one real beauty, Much-Afraid, you have such trustful eyes. Trust is one of the most beautiful things in the world. When I look at the trust in your eyes I find you more beautiful to look upon than many a lovely queen."

In a very short time they were over the bridge, and had come to the foot of the mountains, where the path began the ascent of the lower slopes. Here great boulders were scattered all around, and suddenly Much-Afraid saw the figures of two veiled women seated on one of the rocks at the side of the path. As the Shepherd and she came up to that place, the two rose and bowed silently to him.

"Here are the two guides which I promised," said the Shepherd quietly. "From now on until you are over the steep and difficult places, they will be your companions and helpers."

Much-Afraid looked at them fearfully. Certainly they were tall and appeared to be very strong, but why were they veiled? For what reason did they hide their faces? The longer and closer she looked at them, the more she began to dread them. They were so silent, so strong, and so mysterious. Why did they not speak? Why give her no friendly word of greeting?

"Who are they?" she whispered to the Shepherd. "Will you tell me their names, and why don't they speak to me? Are they dumb?"

"No, they are not dumb," said the Shepherd very quietly, "but they speak a new language, Much-Afraid, a dialect of the mountains which you have not yet learned. But as you travel with them, little by little, you will learn to understand their words.

"They are good teachers; indeed, I have few better. As for their names, I will tell you them in your own language, and later you will learn what they are called in their own tongue. This," said he, motioning toward the first of the silent figures, "is Sorrow. And the other is her twin sister, Suffering."

Poor Much-Afraid! Her cheeks blanched and she began to tremble from head to foot. She felt so like fainting that she clung to the Shepherd for support.

"I can't go with them," she gasped. "I can't! I can't! O my Lord Shepherd, why do you do this to me? How can I travel in their company? It is more than I can bear. You tell me that the mountain way itself is so steep and difficult that I cannot climb it alone. Then why, oh why, must you make Sorrow and Suffering my companions? Couldn't you have given Joy and Peace to go with me, to strengthen me and encourage me and help me on the difficult way? I never thought you would do this to me!" And she burst into tears.

A strange look passed over the Shepherd's face as he listened to this outburst, then looking at the veiled figures as he spoke, he answered very gently, "Joy and Peace. Are those the companions you would choose for yourself? You remember your promise, to accept the helpers that I would give, because you believed that I would choose the very best possible guides for you. Will you still trust me, Much-Afraid? Will you go with them, or do you wish to turn back to the Valley, and to all your Fearing relatives, to Craven Fear himself?"

Much-Afraid shuddered. The choice seemed terrible. Fear she knew only too well, but Sorrow and Suffering had always seemed to her the two most terrifying things which she could encounter. How could she go with them and abandon herself to their power and control? It was impossible. Then she looked at the Shepherd and suddenly knew she could not doubt him, could not possibly turn back from following him; that if she were unfit and unable to love anyone else in the world, yet in her trembling, miserable little heart, she did love him. Even if he asked the impossible, she could not refuse.

She looked at him piteously, then said, "Do I wish to turn back? O Shepherd, to whom should I go? In all the world I have no one but you. Help me to follow you, even though it seems impossible. Help me to trust you as much as I long to love you."

As he heard these words the Shepherd suddenly lifted his head and laughed—a laugh full of exultation and triumph and delight. It echoed round the rocky walls of the little canyon in which they stood until for a moment or two it seemed as though the whole mountain range was laughing with him. The echoes bounded higher and higher, leaping from rock to rock, and from crag to crag, up to the highest summits, until it seemed as though the last faint echoes of it were running into heaven itself.

When the last note had faded into silence, his voice said very softly, "Thou art all fair, my love; there is no spot in thee" (Cant. 4:7). Then he added, "Fear not, Much-Afraid, only believe. I promise that you shall not be put to shame. Go with Sorrow and Suffering, and if you cannot welcome them now, when you come to the difficult places where you cannot manage alone, put your hands in theirs confidently and they will take you exactly where I want you to go."

Much-Afraid stood quite still, looking up into his face, which now had such a happy, exultant look, the look of one who above all things else delights in saving and delivering. In her heart the words of a hymn, written by another of the Shepherd's followers, began to run through her mind and she started to sing softly and sweetly:

Let Sorrow do its work, send grief or pain;
Sweet are thy messengers, sweet their refrain,
If they but work in me, more love, O Christ, to thee,
More love to thee, more love to thee.

"Others have gone this way before me," she thought, "and they could even sing about it afterwards. Will he who is so strong and gentle be less faithful and gracious to me, weak and cowardly though I am, when it is so obvious that the thing he delights in most of all is to deliver his followers from all their fears and to take them to the High Places?" With this came the thought that the sooner she went with these new guides, the sooner she would reach those glorious High Places.

She stepped forward, looking at the two veiled figures, and said with a courage which she had never felt before, "I will go with you. Please lead the way," for even then she could not bring herself to put out her hands to grasp theirs.

The Shepherd laughed again and then said clearly, "My Peace I leave with you. My Joy be fulfilled in you. Remember that I pledge myself to bring you to the High Places at the top of these mountains and that you shall not be put to shame and now 'till the day break and the shadows flee away, I will be like a roe or a young hart on the mountains'" (Cant. 2:17).

Then before Much-Afraid could realize what was happening, he had leaped on to a great rock at the side of the path and from there to another and to yet another, swifter almost than her eyes could follow his movements. He was leaping up the mountains, springing from height to height, going on before them until in a moment or two he was lost to sight.

When they could see him no longer, Much-Afraid and her two new companions began to ascend the foothills. It would have been a curious sight, had there been anyone to watch, as Much-Afraid started on her journey, limping toward the High Places, shrinking as far as possible from the two veiled figures beside her, pretending not to see their proffered hands. But there was no one there to see, for if there is one thing more certain than another, it is that the development of hinds' feet is a secret process, demanding that there should be no onlookers.

Encounter with Pride

FROM THE VERY BEGINNING the way up the mountains proved to be steeper than anything Much-Afraid had supposed herself capable of tackling, and it was not very long before she was forced to seek the help of her companions. Each time she shrinkingly took hold of the hand of either Sorrow or Suffering a pang went through her, but once their hands were grasped she found they had amazing strength, and seemed able to pull and even lift her upwards and over places which she would have considered utterly impossible to reach. Indeed, without their aid they would have been impossible, even for a strong and sure-footed person.

It was not very long, too, before she began to realize how much she needed their help in another way, for it was not only the steepness of the climb and her own lameness and weakness which made the journey difficult. To her surprise and distress she found there were enemies to meet on the way who would certainly have succeeded in making her turn back had she been alone.

To explain this we must now go back to the Valley of Humiliation and see what was happening there. Great was the wrath and consternation of the whole Fearing clan when it was discovered that Much-Afraid had made her escape from the Valley and had actually gone off to the mountains in the company of the Shepherd they so much hated. So long as she had been just ugly, crippled, and miserable little Much-Afraid, her relatives had cared nothing about her. Now they found it quite intolerable that of them all she alone should be singled out in this way and be taken to live on the High Places. Perhaps she would be given service in the palace of the great King himself.

Who was Much-Afraid that this should happen to her while the rest of the family drudged away in the Valley of Humiliation? It was not that they wanted to go to the mountains themselves, far be it, but it was intolerable that Much-Afraid should do so.

So it happened that instead of being a little nobody in the eyes of her relatives, Much-Afraid had suddenly become the central figure in their interest and thought. Not only was her own immediate circle of Fearing relatives concerned about the matter but all of her more distant connections as well. Indeed, the whole population of the Valley, apart from the King's own servants, were angered by her departure, and determined that by some means she must be brought back and the hated Shepherd be robbed of his success in filching her from them.

A great consultation went on between all the more influential relatives, and ways and means discussed by which she could be captured most effectively and be brought back to the Valley as a permanent slave. Finally, it was agreed that someone must be sent after her as quickly as possible in order to force her to return. But they could not conceal from themselves that force might prove impossible, as apparently she had put herself under the protection of the Great Shepherd. Some means, then, would have to be found to beguile her into leaving him of her own free will. How could this be accomplished?

In the end it was unanimously decided to send a distant connection of the family named Pride. The choice fell on him for several reasons. First, he was not only very strong and powerful but was also a handsome young man, and when he chose, could be extremely attractive. It was emphasized that if other means proved unsuccessful he was to feel no scruples against exerting all his powers of fascination in order to coax Much-Afraid away from the Shepherd.

Besides, it was a well-known fact that the young man was by nature far too proud to admit defeat or lack of success in any undertaking, and that there would be no giving up on his part until he accomplished his purpose. As everybody knew, to confess defeat and return without Much-Afraid would be the last thing possible to Pride, so

when he consented to undertake the task it was felt that the matter was as good as settled.

Much-Afraid and her two companions therefore had only been a few days upon their journey and had made but slow though steady progress, when one morning, on turning a corner of the rocky pathway, Pride was seen striding toward them. She was certainly surprised and discomfited at this unexpected apparition, but not unduly alarmed. This cousin had always so disdained and ignored her very existence that at first it never occurred to her that he would even speak to her, but expected to see him pass by in the same haughty manner as usual.

Pride himself, who had been skulking and spying for several hours before he showed himself, was on his part delighted to find that though Much-Afraid seemed to be traveling in the care of two strong companions, yet the Shepherd himself apparently was not with her. He approached her therefore quite confidently but with a most unusual affability of manner, and to Much-Afraid's great surprise stopped when they met, and greeted her.

"Well, Cousin Much-Afraid, here you are at last. I have had such ado to catch up with you."

"How do you do, Cousin Pride?" said that poor little simpleton. Much-Afraid, of course, ought to have known better than to greet, much less to stop and talk with one of her own relatives from the Valley. But it is rather pleasant, after being snubbed and ignored for years, suddenly to be greeted as an equal. Besides this, her curiosity was awakened. Of course, had it been that awful and detestable Craven, nothing would have induced her to stop and speak with him.

"Much-Afraid," said Pride seriously, actually taking her hand in a kindly and friendly manner (it so happened that at that place the path was not quite so steep and she had freed her hands from those of both Sorrow and Suffering), "I have made this journey on purpose to try to help you. I do beg you to allow me to do so and to listen very attentively and seriously.

"My dear cousin, you must give up this extraordinary journey and come back with me to the Valley. You don't realize the true position in which you have put yourself, nor the dreadful future before you. The one who has persuaded you to start this improper journey" (Pride could not bring himself even to mention the Shepherd by name) "is well known to have seduced other helpless victims in this same way.

"Do you know what will happen to you, Much-Afraid, if you persist in going forward? All those fair promises he has made about bringing you into his Kingdom and making you live happily ever afterward will prove false. When he gets you up to the wild, desolate parts of the mountains, he will abandon you altogether, and you will be put to lasting shame."

Poor Much-Afraid tried to pull her hand away, for now she began to understand the meaning of his presence there and his bitter hatred of the Shepherd, but as she struggled to free her hand, he only grasped it tighter. She had to learn that once Pride is listened to, struggle as one may, it is the hardest thing in the world to throw him off. She hated the things that he said, but with her hand grasped in his they had the power to sound horribly plausible and true.

Did she not often find herself in her heart of hearts thrusting back the same idea and possibility which Pride was suggesting to her? Even if the Shepherd did not abandon her (and that she could not believe), might it not be that he who did allow Sorrow and Suffering to be her companions, would also allow her (for her soul's good, of course) to be put to shame before all her relatives and connections? Was she not almost certainly exposing herself to ridicule? Who could know what the Shepherd might allow her to go through (for her ultimate good, perhaps, but quite unbearable to contemplate).

It is a terrible thing to let Pride take one by the hand, Much-Afraid suddenly discovered; his suggestions are so frightfully strong, and through the contact of touch he can press them home with almost irresistible force.

"Come back, Much-Afraid," he urged vehemently. "Give it up before it is too late. In your heart of hearts you know that what I am saying is true and that you will be put to shame before everybody. Give it up while there is still time. Is a merely fictitious promise of living on the High Places worth the cost you are asked to pay for it? What is it that you seek there in that mythological Kingdom above?"

Entirely against her will, and simply because he seemed to have her at his mercy, Much-Afraid let the words be dragged out of her. "I am seeking the Kingdom of Love," she said faintly.

"I thought as much," sneered Pride, "Seeking your heart's desire, eh? And now, Much-Afraid, have a little pride, ask yourself honestly, are you not so ugly and deformed that nobody even in the Valley really loves you? That is the brutal truth. Then how much less will you be welcome in the Kingdom of Love, where they say nothing but unblemished beauty and perfection is admitted? Can you really expect to find what you are seeking; no, I tell you again that you feel this yourself and you know it. Then be honest at least and give it up. Turn back with me before it is too late."

Poor Much-Afraid! The urge to turn back seemed almost irresistible, but at that moment when she stood held in the clutch of Pride, feeling as though every word he spoke was the hideous truth, she had an inner vision of the face of the Shepherd. She remembered the look with which he had promised her, "I pledge myself to bring you there, and that you shall not be put to shame." Then it was as though she heard him again, repeating softly, as though looking at some radiant vision in the distance:

♪ *Behold, thou art fair, my love; thou hast dove's eyes.*
Thou art all fair, my love; there is no spot in thee.

Before Pride could realize what was happening, Much-Afraid uttered a desperate cry for help and was calling up the mountain. "Come to me, Shepherd! Come quickly! Make no tarrying, O my Lord."

There was a sound of loose rattling stones and of a prodigious leap, and the next moment the Shepherd was on the path beside them, his face terrible to look at, his Shepherd's staff raised high above his head. Only one blow fell, and then Pride dropped the hand he had been grasping so tightly and made off down the path and round the corner, slipping and stumbling on the stones as he went, and was out of sight in a moment.

"Much-Afraid," said the Shepherd, in a tone of gentle but firm rebuke, "why did you let Pride come up to you and take your hand? If you had been holding the hands of your two helpers this could never have happened."

For the first time, Much-Afraid of her own free will held out both hands to her two companions, and they grasped her strongly, but never before had their hold upon her been so full of pain, so bitter with sorrow.

She learned in this way the first important lesson on her journey upward, that if one stops to parley with Pride and listens to his poisonous suggestions and, above all, if he is allowed to lay his grasp upon any part of one, Sorrow becomes unspeakably more unbearable afterwards and anguish of heart has bitterness added to it. Moreover, for a while she limped more painfully than ever she had since leaving the Valley. Pride had trodden on her feet at the moment she called for help and left them more lame and sore than ever.

Detour through the Desert

AFTER MEETING PRIDE, Much-Afraid and her companions went on their way, but she was obliged to hobble painfully and could go but slowly. However, she accepted the assistance of her two guides with far greater willingness than before, and gradually the effects of the encounter wore off and she was able to make better progress.

Then one day the path turned a corner, and to her amazement and consternation she saw a great plain spread out beneath them. As far as the eye could see there seemed to be nothing but desert, and endless expanse of sand dunes, with not a tree in sight. The only objects breaking the monotony of the desert were strange, towering pyramids, rising above the sand dunes, hoary with age and grimly desolate. To the horror of Much-Afraid her two guides prepared to take the steep path downwards.

She stopped dead and said to them, "We mustn't go down there. The Shepherd has called me to the High Places. We must find some path which goes up, but certainly not down there." But they made signs to her that she was to follow them down the steep pathway to the desert below.

Much-Afraid looked to left and right, but though it seemed incredible, there was no way possible by which they could continue to climb upward. The hill they were on ended abruptly at this precipice, and the rocky cliffs towered above them in every direction straight as walls with no possible foothold.

"I can't go down there," panted Much-Afraid, sick with shock and fear. "He can never mean that—never! He called me up to the High Places, and this is an absolute contradiction of all that he promised."

She then lifted up her voice and called desperately, "Shepherd, come to me. Oh, I need you. Come and help me."

In a moment he was there, standing beside her.

"Shepherd," she said despairingly, "I can't understand this. The guides you gave me say that we must go down there into that desert, turning right away from the High

Places altogether. You don't mean that, do you? You can't contradict yourself. Tell them we are not to go there, and show us another way. Make a way for us, Shepherd, as you promised."

He looked at her and answered very gently, "That is the path, Much-Afraid, and you are to go down there."

"Oh, no," she cried. "You can't mean it. You said if I would trust you, you would bring me to the High Places, and that path leads right away from them. It contradicts all that you promised."

"No," said the Shepherd, "it is not contradiction, only postponement for the best to become possible."

Much-Afraid felt as though he had stabbed her to the heart. "You mean," she said incredulously, "you really mean that I am to follow that path down and down into that wilderness and then over that desert, away from the mountains indefinitely? Why" (and there was a sob of anguish in her voice) "it may be months, even years, before that path leads back to the mountains again. O Shepherd, do you mean it is indefinite postponement?"

He bowed his head silently, and Much-Afraid sank on her knees at his feet, almost overwhelmed. He was leading her away from her heart's desire altogether and gave no promise at all as to when he would bring her back. As she looked out over what seemed an endless desert, the only

path she could see led farther and farther away from the High Places, and it was all desert.

Then he answered very quietly, "Much-Afraid, do you love me enough to accept the postponement and the apparent contradiction of the promise, and to go down there with me into the desert?"

She was still crouching at his feet, sobbing as if her heart would break, but now she looked up through her tears, caught his hand in hers, and said, trembling, "I do love you, you know that I love you. Oh, forgive me because I can't help my tears. I will go down with you into the wilderness, right away from the promise, if you really wish it. Even if you cannot tell me why it has to be, I will go with you, for you know I do love you, and you have the right to choose for me anything that you please."

It was very early morning, and high above them, hanging in the sky over the silent expanse of desert, was a young crescent moon and the morning star shining like a brilliant jewel close beside it. There Much-Afraid built her first altar on the mountains, a little pile of broken rocks, and then, with the Shepherd standing close beside her, she laid down on the altar her trembling, rebelling will. A littler spurt of flame came from somewhere, and in an instant nothing but a heap of ashes was lying on the altar. That is to say, she thought at first there were only ashes, but the Shepherd told her to look closer, and there among the ashes she saw a little stone of some kind, a dark-colored, common-looking pebble.

"Pick it up and take it with you," said the Shepherd gently, "as a memorial of this altar which you built, and all that it stands for."

Much-Afraid took the stone out of the ashes, scarcely looking at it and feeling that to her life's end she would never need a reminder of that altar, for how could she ever forget it or the anguish of that first surrender, but she dropped the pebble into a little purse or bag which the Shepherd gave her and put it away carefully.

Then they began the descent into the desert, and at the first step Much-Afraid felt a thrill of the sweetest joy and comfort surge through her, for she found that the Shepherd himself was going down with them. She would not have Sorrow and Suffering as her only companions, but he was there too. As she started down the path he began a song which Much-Afraid had not heard before, and it sounded so sweet and comforting that her pain began to melt away. It was as though the song suggested to her a part at least of the reason for this strange postponement of all her hopes. This is the song he sang:

THE CLOSED GARDEN

A garden closed art thou, my love,
Where none thy fruits can taste,
A spring shut up, a fountain sealed,
An orchard run to waste.
Awake north wind!
And come, thou south!
Blow on my garden fair,
That all the spices may flow out
As perfume on the air.

CANT. 4:12-16

They reached the desert surprisingly quickly, because, although the path was very steep indeed, Much-Afraid was leaning on the Shepherd, and did not feel her weakness at all. By the evening of that same day they were down on the pale sand dunes and walking toward some huts built in the shadow of one of the great pyramids, where they were to rest that night. At sunset, when the sky burned fiery red over the western rim of the desert, the Shepherd led Much-Afraid away from the huts, to the foot of the pyramid.

"Much-Afraid," he said, "all of my servants on their way to the High Places have had to make this detour through the desert. It is called 'The furnace of Egypt, and an horror of great darkness' (Gen. 15:12, 17). Here they have learned many things which otherwise they would have known nothing about.

"Abraham was the first of my servants to come this way, and this pyramid was hoary with age when he first looked upon it. Then came Joseph, with tears and anguish of heart, and looked upon it too and learned the lesson of the furnace of fire. Since that time an endless succession of my people have come this way. They came to learn the secret of royalty, and now you are here, Much-Afraid. You, too, are in the line of succession. It is a great privilege, and if you will, you also may learn the lesson of the furnace and of the great darkness just as surely as did those before you. Those who come down to the furnace go on their way afterwards as royal men and women, princes and princesses of the Royal Line."

Much-Afraid looked up at the towering pyramid, now shadowy and black against the sunset sky, and desolate as it looked in the waste of desert, yet it seemed to her to be one of the most majestic objects she had ever seen.

Then all of a sudden the desert was full of people, an endless procession of them. There was Abraham himself and Sarah his wife, those first lonely exiles in a strange land; there was Joseph, the betrayed and wounded brother who had been sold into slavery, who when he wept for his

MEMORIAL STONE № 1

As you join Much-Afraid on this journey, record memorial stones you collect along the way.

painful to surrender my will
is he the right path? will I
be led astray? God.. Show me

Am I praying for the wrong things?

father's tent, saw only the alien pyramid. Then one after another she saw a great host which no man could number stretching across the desert in an endless line. The last one in the line held out a hand which she took, and there she was in the great chain herself. Words came to her ears also, and she heard them quite plainly.

"Fear not, Much-Afraid, to go down into Egypt; for I will there make of thee a great nation; I will go down with thee into Egypt; and I will also surely bring thee up again" (Gen. 46:3-4).

After this they went back to the huts to rest that night. In the morning the Shepherd called Much-Afraid again and led her away, but this time he opened a little door in the wall of the pyramid and took her inside. There was a passage which led to the center, and from there a spiral staircase went up to the floors above.

But the Shepherd opened another door leading out of the central chamber on the ground floor and they entered a very large room which looked like a granary. There were great piles of grain everywhere except in the middle. There on the open space men were threshing the different kinds of grain in many different ways and then grinding them to powder, some coarse and some finer. At one side were women sitting on the ground with hollow smooth stones before them, grinding the very best of the wheat into the finest possible powder.

Watching them for a while, Much-Afraid saw how the grains were first beaten and bruised until they crumbled to pieces, but still the grinding and beating process continued, until at last the powder was fine enough to be used for baking the best wheat bread.

"See," said the Shepherd gently, "how various are the methods used for grinding the different varieties of grain, according to their special use and purpose." Then he quoted, "Dill is not threshed with a threshing instrument, neither is a cart wheel turned about upon the cummin; but dill is beaten out with a staff, and the cummin with a rod. Bread corn is bruised, but no one crushes it forever; neither is it broken with the wheel of a cart nor bruised with horsemen driving over it" (Isa. 28:27-28).

As Much-Afraid watched the women pounding the bread corn with their heavy stones she noticed how long the process took before the fine white powder was finished and ready for use. Then she heard the Shepherd saying, "I bring my people into Egypt that they, too, may be threshed and ground into the finest powder and may become bread corn for the use of others. But remember, though bread corn is bruised, no one threshes it for ever; only until the bruised and broken grain is ready for its highest use. This also cometh forth from the Lord of Hosts, which is wonderful in counsel and excellent in working" (v. 29).

After this the Shepherd took her back to the central chamber and they ascended the spiral staircase, twisting up and up into the darkness above. There, on the next floor, they came to another and smaller room, in the center of which stood a great wheel, flat, like a table. Beside it stood a potter who wrought a work on the wheel. As he spun the wheel he fashioned his clay into many beautiful shapes and objects. The material was cut and kneaded and shaped as he saw fit, but always the clay lay still upon the wheel, submitting to his every touch, perfectly, unresisting.

As they watched, the Shepherd said, "In Egypt, too, I fashion my fairest and finest vessels and bring forth instruments for my work, according as I see fit" (Jer. 18). Then he smiled and added, "Cannot I do with you, Much-Afraid, as this potter? Behold, as the clay is in the hand of the potter so are you in my hand" (Jer. 18:6).

Last of all he took her up the stairway to the highest floor. There they found a room with a furnace in which gold was being smelted and refined of all its dross. Also in

The Good Shepherd is the potter and you are his clay. Reflect
on the ways the Good Shepherd is fashioning you into a fine vessel.
Be willing to let him shape, mold, and refine you for his glory.

_____

_____

_____

_____

the furnace were rough pieces of stone and rock containing crystals. These were put in the great heat of the oven and left for a time. On being taken out, behold, they were glorious jewels, flashing as though they had received the fire into their very hearts. As Much-Afraid stood beside the Shepherd, looking shrinkingly into the fire, he said the loveliest thing of all.

"O thou afflicted, tossed with tempest, and not comforted, behold, I will lay thy stones with fair colors, and lay thy foundations with sapphires. And I will make thy windows of agates, and thy gates of carbuncles, and all thy borders of pleasant stones" (Isa. 54:11-12). Then he added, "My rarest and choicest jewels and my finest gold are those who have been refined in the furnace of Egypt," and he sang one verse of a little song:

I'll turn my hands upon thy heart,
And purge away thy dross,
I will refine thee in my fire
Remake thee at my cross.

They stayed at the huts in the desert for several days, and Much-Afraid learned many things which she had never heard before.

One thing, however, made a special impression upon her. In all that great desert, there was not a single green thing growing, neither tree nor flower nor plant save here and there a patch of straggly grey cacti.

On the last morning she was walking near the tents and huts of the desert dwellers, when in a lonely corner behind a wall she came upon a little golden-yellow flower, growing all alone. An old pipe was connected with a water tank. In the pipe was one tiny hole through which came an occasional drop of water. Where the drops fell one by one, there grew the little golden flower, though where the seed had come from, Much-Afraid could not imagine, for there were no birds anywhere and no other growing things.

She stopped over the lonely, lovely little golden face lifted up so hopefully and so bravely to the feeble drip, and cried out softly, "What is your name, little flower, for I never saw one like you before."

The tiny plant answered at once in a tone as golden as itself, "Behold me! My name is Acceptance-with-Joy."

Much-Afraid thought of the things which she had seen in the pyramid: the threshing-floor and the whirring wheel and the fiery furnace. Somehow the answer of the little golden flower which grew all alone in the waste of the desert stole into her heart and echoed there faintly but sweetly, filling her with comfort. She said to herself, "He has brought me here when I did not want to come for his own purpose. I, too, will look up into his face and say, 'Behold me! I am thy little handmaiden Acceptance-with-Joy.'" Then she stooped down and picked up a pebble which was lying in the sand beside the flower and put it in the purse with the first altar stone.

MEMORIAL STONE Nº 2
How could I forget that You
give/bring me peace?
& That you are REFINING ME??
I want to be like the little golden
flower.

On the Shores of Loneliness

AFTER THEY WALKED TOGETHER through the burning desert sands, then one day, quite unexpectedly, a path crossed the main track which they were following. "This," said the Shepherd quietly, "is the path which you are now to follow." So they turned westward with the High Places right behind their backs and came in a little while to the end of the desert. They found themselves on the shore of a great sea.

"It is now time for me to leave you, Much-Afraid," he said, "and to return to the mountains. Remember, even though you seem to be farther away than ever from the High Places and from me, there is really no distance at all separating us. I can cross the desert sands as swiftly as I can leap from the High Places to the valleys, and whenever you call for me, I shall come. This is the word I now leave with you. Believe it and practice it with joy. My sheep hear my voice and they follow me.

"Whenever you are willing to obey me, Much-Afraid, and to follow the path of my choice, you will always be able to hear and recognize my voice, and when you hear it you must always obey. Remember also that it is always safe to obey my voice, even if it seems to call you to paths which look impossible or even crazy." On saying this he blessed her and went from them, leaping and bounding over the desert toward the High Places, which were now actually right behind her.

Much-Afraid and her two companions walked along the shores of the great sea for many days, and at first it seemed to her that up till then she had never known real loneliness.

The green valley where all her friends and she had lived was far away behind her. Even the mountains were out of sight, and there seemed to be nothing in the whole wide world but the endless sandy desert on one side and the endless sea moaning drearily on the other. Nothing grew there, neither tree nor shrub nor even grass, but the shores were scattered with broken driftwood and with great tangled masses of brown and shriveled seaweed. Nothing lived in the whole region save the sea gulls wheeling and crying overhead and the crabs scuttling across the sand into their burrows. At intervals, too, an icy wind came shrilling across the billows, stabbing sharp as a knife.

In those days Much-Afraid never let go the hands of her two companions, and it was amazing how swiftly they helped her along. Stranger still, perhaps, was the way in which Much-Afraid walked, swifter and more upright than ever before, and with scarcely a limp, for something had happened in the wilderness which had left a mark upon her for the rest of her life. It was an inner and secret mark, and no one would have noticed any difference outwardly, but all the same, a deep inner change had taken place which indicated a new stage in her life.

She had been down into Egypt and had looked upon the grinding-stones, the wheel, and the furnace, and knew that they symbolized an experience which she herself must pass through. Somehow, incredible as it was, she, Much-Afraid, had been enabled to accept the knowledge and to acquiesce in it, and she knew within herself that with that acceptance a gulf had opened between herself and her past life, even between her past self; a gulf which could never again be closed.

She could look back across it to the green valley between the mountains and see herself there with the Shepherd's workers, feeding her little flock, cringing before her relatives and going to the pool morning and evening to keep tryst with the Shepherd. But it was looking at somebody else together, and she said to herself, "I was that woman, but am not that woman now."

She did not understand how it happened, but what the Shepherd had said had come to pass in herself, for those who go down into the furnace of Egypt and find there the flower of Acceptance come up changed and with the stamp of royalty upon them. It is true that Much-Afraid did not feel at all royal, and certainly did not as yet look it. Nevertheless, she had been stamped with the mark, and would never be the same again.

Therefore, though she went with Sorrow and Suffering day after day along the shores of the great sea of Loneliness, she did not go cringingly or complainingly. Indeed, gradually an impossible thing seemed to be happening. A new kind of joy was springing up in her heart, and she began to find herself noticing beauties in the landscape of which until then she had been quite unconscious.

Her heart often thrilled with an inner ecstasy when she caught sight of the sun shining on the wings of the wheeling sea-gulls, making them gleam as dazzlingly white as the snow on the peaks of the far-off High Places. Even their wild, mournful cries and the moanings of the water stirred in her a sorrow which was strangely beautiful. She had the feeling that somehow, in the very far-off places, perhaps even in far-off ages, there would be a meaning found to all sorrow and an answer too fair and wonderful to be as yet understood.

Often, too, she found herself laughing aloud as she watched the antics of the funny little scuttling crabs. When the sun shone brightly, as it did at times, even the grey, dreary sea was transformed into a thing of surpassing beauty, with the light gleaming on the curving green breakers and the foaming spray and the horizon blue as a midnight sky. When the sun thus shone on the wild wastes of waters it seemed as though all their sorrows had been swallowed up in joy, and then she would whisper to herself, "When he hath tried me, I shall come forth as gold. Weeping may endure for a night, but joy cometh in the morning."

One day they came to a place on the shore where were high cliffs and great rocks scattered all about. In this place they were to rest for a time, and while there Much-Afraid wandered off by herself. After climbing the cliff she found herself looking down into a lonely little cove completely enclosed on three sides by the cliffs and with nothing in it but driftwood and stranded seaweed. The chief impression it made upon her was its emptiness. It seemed to lie there like an empty heart, watching and longing for the far-off tide which had receded to such a distance that it could never again return.

When, however, drawn by an urge to revisit the lonely cove, Much-Afraid went back to the same spot some hours later, all was changed. The waves were now rushing forward with the strength of a high tide urging them onward. Looking over the edge of the cliff, she saw that the cove which had been so empty was now filled to the brim. Great waves, roaring and laughing together, were pouring themselves through the narrow inlet and were leaping against the sides, irresistibly taking possession of every empty niche and crevice.

On seeing this transformation, she knelt down on the edge of the cliff and built her third altar. "O my Lord," she cried, "I thank thee for leading me here. Behold me, here I am, empty as was this little cove, but waiting thy time to be filled to the brim with the flood-tide of Love." Then she picked up a little piece of quartz and crystal which was lying on the rocky cliff and dropped it beside the other memorial stones in the little bag which she carried with her.

It was only a short time after the building of that new altar that her enemies were all upon her again. Far away in the Valley of Humiliation, her relatives had been awaiting the return of Pride with his victim, but as time passed and he did not return and Much-Afraid did not reappear

 MEMORIAL STONE № 3

it became obvious that he must have been unsuccessful in his undertaking and was too proud to admit it. They decided that reinforcements must be sent as soon as possible, before Much-Afraid could reach the really High Places and be altogether beyond their reach.

Spies were sent out, who met Pride and brought back word that Much-Afraid was nowhere on the mountains but was far away on the shores of the Sea of Loneliness. She was going in quite a different direction from the mountains altogether. This was unexpectedly delightful and encouraging news, and quickly suggested to them the best reinforcements to be sent to the help of Pride. There was complete unanimity in deciding that Resentment, Bitterness, and Self-Pity should hurry off at once to assist in bringing back Much-Afraid to her eagerly-awaiting relatives.

Off they went to the shores of Loneliness, and Much-Afraid now had to endure a time of really dreadful assaults. It is true that her enemies soon discovered that this was not the same Much-Afraid with whom they had to deal. They could never get within close reach, because she kept so near to Sorrow and Suffering and accepted their assistance so much more willingly than before. However, they kept appearing before her, shouting out their horrid suggestions and mocking her until it really seemed that wherever she went one or another popped up (there were so many hiding-places for them among the rocks) and hurled their darts at her.

"I told you so," Pride would shout viciously. "Where are you now, you little fool? Up on the High Places: Not much! Do you know that everyone in the Valley of Humiliation knows about this and is laughing at you? Seeking your heart's desire, eh, and left abandoned by him

(just as I warned you) on the shores of Loneliness. Why didn't you listen to me, you little fool?"

Then Resentment would raise his head over another rock. He was extremely ugly to look at, but his was a horribly fascinating ugliness. Sometimes Much-Afraid could hardly turn her eyes away when he stared at her boldly and shouted, "You know, Much-Afraid, you act like a blind idiot. Who is this Shepherd you follow? What sort of a person is he to demand everything you have and take everything you offer and give nothing in return but suffering and sorrow and ridicule and shame? Why do you let him treat you like this? Stand up for yourself and demand that he fulfill his promise and take you at once to the High Places. If not, tell him that you feel absolved from all necessity to follow him any longer."

Bitterness would then break in with his sneering voice, "The more you yield to him, the more he will demand from you. He is cruel to you, and takes advantage of your devotion. All he has demanded from you so far is nothing to what he will demand if you persist in following him. He lets his followers, yes, even women and children, go to concentration camps and torture chambers and hideous deaths of all kinds. Could you bear that, you little whiner? Then you'd better pull out and leave him before he demands the uttermost sacrifice of all. Sooner or later, he'll put you on a cross of some sort and abandon you to it."

Self-Pity would chime in next, and in some dreadful way he was almost worse than any of the others. He talked so softly and in such a pitying tone that Much-Afraid would feel weak all over.

"Poor little Much-Afraid," he would whisper. "It is too bad, you know. You really are so devoted, and you have refused him nothing, absolutely nothing; yet this is the cruel way in which he treats you. Can you really believe when he acts toward you like this that he loves you and has your real good at heart? How can that be possible?

"You have every right to feel sorry for yourself. Even if you are perfectly willing to suffer for his sake, at least other people ought to know about it and pity you instead of misunderstanding and ridiculing as they do. It really seems as though the one you follow takes delight in making you suffer and leaving you to be misunderstood, for every time you yield to him he thinks up some new way of wounding and bruising you."

That last remark of Self-Pity's was a mistake, because the word "bruising" suddenly reminded Much-Afraid of what the Shepherd had said when they stood together on the threshing-floor in the Pyramid. "Bread corn is bruised," he had said, "but no one threshes it forever, only till it is ready to be made bread for others. This also cometh forth from the LORD of Hosts who is wonderful in counsel and excellent in working" (Isa. 28:28-29).

When she thought of this, to Self-Pity's dismayed astonishment, Much-Afraid actually picked up a piece of rock and hurled it at him, and as he said afterwards to the other three in an aggrieved tone of voice, "If I hadn't ducked and bolted like a hare it could have laid me out altogether, the little vixen!"

But it is exhausting to be assaulted day after day with suggestions like these, and while Sorrow and Suffering were holding her hands, naturally Much-Afraid could not

cover her ears, so her enemies were really able to give her a dreadful time. At last, things came to a crisis.

One day when her companions actually seemed to be sleeping for a little while, Much-Afraid unwarily wandered off alone. Not this time to her favorite spot looking down into the little cove, but in a new direction, and she came to a place where the cliffs jutted out into the sea, forming a very narrow peninsula, which ended in a sheer precipice.

When she reached the end of this promontory she stood looking out over the endless expanse of sea, and suddenly found to her horror all four of her enemies approaching and closing in on her. That already she was becoming a different person was then quite apparent, for instead of nearly fainting with fright at their approach, although she did look very pale and frightened, she actually seized a stone in each hand and, putting her back against a great rock, prepared to resist them to the limit of her strength.

Fortunately the place was too narrow for all four to approach together, but Pride put himself in front of the others and stepped toward her holding a strong cudgel.

"You can put down those stones, Much-Afraid," said he savagely. "There are four of us here, and we mean to do as we please with you now that you are in our power. You shall not only listen to us but shall go with us."

Much-Afraid lifted her face toward the seemingly empty sky, and with all her strength called out, "Come to my deliverance and make no tarrying, O my Lord."

To the horror of the four ruffians, there was the

Shepherd himself, leaping toward them along the narrow promontory more terrible than a great mountain stag with thrusting horns. Resentment, Bitterness, and Self-Pity managed to hurl themselves flat on the ground and edge away as he bounded toward the place where Pride was just seizing hold of Much-Afraid. Catching him by the shoulders, the Shepherd spun him around, lifted him in the air, where he uttered a loud, despairing shriek, and then dropped him over the edge of the cliff into the sea.

"O Shepherd," gasped Much-Afraid, shaking with relief and hope, "thank you. Do you think Pride is really dead at last?"

"No," said the Shepherd, "it is most unlikely." He glanced over the cliff as he spoke, and caught sight of Pride swimming like a fish toward the shore, and added, "There he goes, but he has had a fall today which he will not forget, and I fancy he will limp for some time to come. As for the other three, they have made off into some hiding place, and are not likely to trouble you again in the same way now that they realize that I am within call."

"Shepherd," asked Much-Afraid earnestly, "tell me why I nearly got into Pride's clutches again, and why Resentment, Bitterness, and Self-Pity have been able to pester me for so long in this dreadful way. I did not call you before, because they never dared to come close to me or to make a real attack, but they have been lurking around all the time and making their horrible suggestions, and I couldn't get away from them. Why was it?"

"I think," said the Shepherd gently, "that lately the way seemed a little easier and the sun shone, and you came to a place where you could rest. You forgot for a while that you were my little handmaiden Acceptance-with-Joy and were beginning to tell yourself it really was time that I led you back to the mountains and up to the High Places. When you wear the weed of impatience in your heart instead of the flower Acceptance-with-Joy, you will always find your enemies get an advantage over you."

Much-Afraid blushed. She knew how right he was in his diagnosis. It had been easier to accept the hard path and to be patient when the sea was grey and dull than now when the sun shone and everything else around looked bright and happy and satisfied. She put her hand in the Shepherd's and said sorrowfully, "You are quite right. I have been thinking that you are allowing me to follow this path too long and that you were forgetting your promise." Then she added, looking steadfastly into his face, "But I do tell you now with all my heart that you are my Shepherd whose voice I love to hear and obey, and that it is my joy to follow you. You choose, my Lord, and I will obey."

The Shepherd stooped down and picked up a stone which was lying beside her feet and said smilingly, "Put this in your bag with the other stones as a memorial of this day when for the first time you saw Pride toppled over before you, and of your promise that you will wait patiently until I give you your heart's desire."

 MEMORIAL STONE № 4

On the Old Sea Wall

A FEW DAYS HAD PASSED after the victory over Pride, and Much-Afraid and her companions were continuing their journey along the shore of the great sea. One morning the path unexpectedly turned inland again and they found themselves facing back over the desert in the direction of the mountains, although, of course, they were too far away to be visible. With a thrill of indescribable joy Much-Afraid saw that at last the path did actually run straight toward the east and that it would lead them back to the High Places.

She dropped the hands of her two guides in order to clap her own, and gave a little skip of joy. No matter how great the distance between them and the mountains, now at last they were to go in the right direction. All three started back across the desert, but Much-Afraid could not wait for her guides, and actually ran on ahead as though she had never been lame at all.

Suddenly the path took another turn at right angles and went straight before her as far as she could see, not toward the mountains at all, but southward again to where far ahead the desert seemed to end in some sort of hill country. Much-Afraid stood quite still, dumb with

dismay and shock. Then she began to tremble all over. It could not be possible, no, it couldn't, that yet again the Shepherd was saying "No," and turning her right away from the High Places.

"Hope deferred maketh the heart sick," said the wise man of long ago, and how truly he spoke! Now she had been skipping and running so excitedly along the path toward the mountains that she had left Sorrow and Suffering quite behind, and while they were catching up with her she was standing quite alone at the place where the path turned away from the mountains.

Up from behind a sand dune close beside her rose the form of her enemy Bitterness. He did not come any nearer, having learned a little more prudence, and was not going to make her call for the Shepherd if he could avoid it, but simply stood and looked at her and laughed and laughed again, the bitterest sound that Much-Afraid had heard in all her life.

Then he said, as venomously as a viper, "Why don't you laugh too, you little fool? You knew this would happen." There he stood, uttering these awful bursts of laughter until it seemed that the whole desert was filled with the echoes of his mockery. Sorrow and her sister came up to Much-Afraid and stood by her side quite silently, and for a little while everything was swallowed up in pains and "an horror of great darkness." A sudden swirling wind shrieked over the desert and raised a storm of dust and sand which blinded them.

In the silence which succeeded the storm Much-Afraid heard her voice, low and trembling, but quite distinct, saying, "My Lord, what dost thou want to say to me? Speak—for thy servant heareth."

Next moment the Shepherd was standing beside her. "Be of good cheer," he said, "it is I, be not afraid. Build me another altar and lay down your whole will as a burnt offering."

Obediently Much-Afraid raised a little heap of sand and loose stones, which was all that she could find in the desert, and again laid down her will and said with tears (for Sorrow had stepped forward and knelt beside her), "I delight to do thy will, O my God."

From somewhere, though they could not see the source, there came a spurt of flame which consumed the offering and left a little heap of ashes on the altar. Then came the Shepherd's voice. "This further delay is not unto death, but for the glory of God; that the son of God may be glorified."

Another gust of wind sprang up and whirled the ashes away in every direction, and the only thing remaining on the altar was a rough, ordinary-looking stone which Much-Afraid picked up and put into the bag with the others. Then she rose to her feet, turned her face away from the mountains, and they all started southward. The Shepherd went with them for a little way so that Resentment and Self-Pity, who were hiding close at hand awaiting an opportunity to attack, lay flat behind the sand dunes and were not seen at that time at all.

Presently they reached a place where the sea, which they had left behind when they turned inland, came sweeping into the desert, forming a great estuary. A strong tide was surging into it, filling it completely with swiftly-flowing waters. However, a stone causeway with many arches had been built across the estuary, and an earthen ramp led up to it. The Shepherd led Much-Afraid to the foot of the ramp and told her to follow this path across the sea. Once more he repeated with great emphasis the words which he had spoken beside the altar, then departed.

Much-Afraid, followed by her two companions, scrambled up the ramp and found themselves on top of the old sea wall. From the height on which they now stood they could look back over the desert. On one side was the sea, and on the other, so blurred with distance that they could not be sure if they really saw it, was a haze which might be part of the mountains, or was it only wishful thinking?

Then, looking ahead they saw that the causeway would indeed bring them across the estuary into a different kind of country altogether, a well-wooded land of hills and valleys with cottages and farmsteads among orchards and fields. The sun was shining brilliantly, and up there on the wall they could feel the full force of the great wind which was urging and lashing the rushing waves to flow swifter and swifter. It reminded Much-Afraid of a pack of hounds, urged on by the huntsmen, following one another, leaping and surging and roaring beneath the causeway and then flowing forward far inland, brimming the shores of the estuary.

Somehow the roar of the wind and the surge of the waters seemed to get into her blood and course through her being like a glorious wine of life. The wind whipped her cheeks and tore at her hair and clothes and nearly toppled her over, but she stood there, shouting at the

AND NOW SHALL MINE HEAD BE LIFTED UP ABOVE ...II MINE ENEMIES WILL SING PRAISES UNTO THE LORD.

PSALM 27:6

top of her voice, though the wind seized the sound of it and carried it off, crowned in a deafening roar of its own. What Much-Afraid was shouting up there on the old sea wall was this:

"And now shall mine head be lifted up above mine enemies round about; therefore I will sing praises unto the Lord; yea I will offer the sacrifice of joy and will praise the Name of the Lord" (Psa. 27:6).

As she sang she thought to herself, "It must be really dreadful to be the Shepherd's enemies. Always, always to find themselves frustrated. Always, always to have their prey snatched away. How simply maddening it must be to see even the silliest little weaklings set up out of reach on the High Places and made to triumph over all their enemies. It must be unbearable."

While still on the causeway she picked up another stone as the Shepherd had taught her, this time as a memorial of his victory in making her triumph over her enemies, and dropped it into the little bag of treasured memories. So they made their way across the causeway and down the ramp on the other side and immediately found themselves in a wood.

The change in scene after their long journey through the desert was wonderful. A long-deferred spring was just loosening everything from the grip of winter, and all the trees were bursting into fairest green and the buds were swelling. In between the trees were glades of bluebells and wild anemones, and violets and primroses grew in clumps along the mossy banks. Birds sang and called to one another and rustled about, busily absorbed in nest-building.

Much-Afraid told herself that never before had she realized what the awakening from the death of winter was like. Perhaps it had needed the desert wastes to open her eyes to all this beauty, but she walked through the wood, almost forgetting for a little that Sorrow and her sister also walked with her.

Everywhere she looked it seemed that the unfurling green on the trees and the nesting birds and the leaping squirrels and blossoming flowers were all saying the same thing, greeting one another in their own special language with a sort of ecstasy and calling cheerfully, "You see, the winter has gone at last. The delay was not unto death but for the glory of God. Never was there a fairer spring than this."

At the same time Much-Afraid herself was conscious of a wonderful stirring in her own heart, as though something were springing up and breaking into new life there too. The feeling was so sweet, yet so mixed with pain that she hardly knew which predominated. She thought of the seed of Love which the Shepherd had planted in her heart, and half-afraid and half-eager, she looked to see if it had really taken root and was springing up. She saw a mass of leaves, and at the end of the stem a little swelling which might almost prove to be a bud.

As Much-Afraid looked at it another stab went through her heart, for she remembered the words of the Shepherd that when the plant of Love was ready to bloom she would be loved in return and would receive a new name up there on the High Places. But here she was, still far away from them, indeed farther than ever before, and with apparently no possibility of going there for a long time to come. How could the Shepherd's promise prove true? When she thought of that her tears fell again.

 MEMORIAL STONE N⁰ 5

You may think that Much-Afraid was altogether too much given to shedding tears, but remember that she had Sorrow for a companion and teacher. There is this to be added, that her tears were all in secret, for no one but her enemies knew about this strange journey on which she had set out. The heart knoweth its own sorrow and there are times when, like David, it is comforting to think that our tears are put in a bottle and not one of them forgotten by the one who leads us in paths of sorrow.

But she did not weep for long, for almost at once she caught sight of something else, a gleam of gold. Looking closer, what should she see but an exact replica of the little golden flower which she had found growing near the pyramids in the desert. Somehow it had been transplanted and was actually growing in her own heart. Much-Afraid gave a cry of delight, and the tiny golden thing nodded and said in its little golden voice, "Behold me, here I am, growing in your heart, 'Acceptance-with-Joy.'"

Much-Afraid smiled and answered, "Why, yes, of course, I was forgetting," and she knelt down there in the wood, put a pile of stones together and laid sticks on them. As you have noticed, altars are built of whatever materials lie close at hand at the time. Then she hesitated. What should she lay on the altar this time? She looked at the tiny swelling on the plant of Love which might be a bud and again might not, then she leaned forward, placed her heart on the altar and said, "Behold me, here I am; thy little handmaiden Acceptance-with-Joy and all that is in my heart is thine."

This time, though there came a flame of fire and burned up the sticks, the bud was still on the stem of the plant. Perhaps, thought Much-Afraid, because it was too small to offer. But nevertheless something lovely had happened. It was as though a spark from the flame had entered her heart and was still glowing there, warm and radiant. On the altar among the ashes was yet another stone for her to pick up and put with the rest, so now there were six stones of remembrance lying in the bag she carried. Going on their way, in a very short time they came to the edge of the wood and she uttered a cry of joy, for who should be standing there, waiting to meet them, but the Shepherd himself. She ran toward him as though she had wings on her feet.

"Oh, welcome, welcome, a thousand times welcome!" cried Much-Afraid, tingling with joy from head to foot. "I am afraid there is nothing much in the garden of my heart as yet, Shepherd, but all that there is, is yours to do with as you please."

"I have come to bring you a message," said the Shepherd. "You are to be ready, Much-Afraid, for something new. This is the message, 'Now shalt thou see what I will do'" (Ex. 6:1).

The color leaped into her cheeks, and a shock of joy went through her, for she remembered the plant in her heart and the promise that when it was ready to bloom she would be up on the High Places and ready to enter the Kingdom of Love.

"O Shepherd," she exclaimed, almost breathless with the thought. "Do you mean that I am really to go the High Places at last? Really—at last?"

She thought he nodded, but he did not answer at once, but stood looking at her with an expression she did not quite understand.

"Do you mean it?" she repeated, catching his hand and looking up at him with almost incredulous joy. "Do you mean you soon will be taking me to the High Places?"

This time he answered, "Yes," and added with a strange smile, "now shalt thou see what I will do."

Great Precipice Injury

AFTER THAT, FOR A LITTLE WHILE Much-Afraid had a song in her heart as she walked among the fields and orchards and the low hills of the country to which they had come. It hardly seemed to matter now that Sorrow and Suffering were still with her because of the hope leaping up in her heart that soon they would cease to be her companions altogether, for when she came to the mountains again and they had helped her up to the High Places she would need them no longer. Neither did it matter that the path they followed still led southward, twisting among the hills and leading through quiet valleys, because she had the Shepherd's own promise that soon it would lead her back to the eastern mountains and to the place of her heart's desire.

After a time the path began sloping upward toward the summits of the hills.

One day they suddenly reached the top of the highest of the hills and just as the sun rose found themselves on a great plateau. They looked eastward toward the golden sunrise, and Much-Afraid burst into a cry of joy and thankfulness. There, at no great distance, on the farther side of the plateau, were the mountains, quite distinct and rising like a great wall, crowned with ramparts and towers and pinnacles, all of which were glowing rose-red and gold in the sunrise. Never, thought she, had she seen anything so beautiful.

As the sun rose higher and the glow faded from the sky, she saw that the highest peaks were covered with snow, so white and glittering that her eyes were dazzled with their glory. She was looking at the High Places themselves. Best of all, the path they were following here turned eastward and led directly toward the mountains.

Much-Afraid fell on her knees on the hilltop, bowed her head and worshiped. It seemed to her at that moment that all the pain and the postponement, all the sorrows and trials of the long journey she had made, were as nothing compared to the glory which shone before her. It seemed to her, too, that even her companions were smiling with her. When she had worshiped and rejoiced she rose to her feet and all three started to cross the plateau. It was amazing how quickly they went, for the path was flat and comparatively smooth, and before they could have believed it possible they found themselves approaching the mountains and were among the slopes and boulders at their very feet.

As they approached, Much-Afraid could not help

being struck by the steepness of these slopes, and the nearer they drew, the more like impassable walls the mountains appeared to become. But she told herself that when she was right up to them they would find a valley or gorge, or a pass up which they could proceed, and that she certainly would not mind how steep the way was if only it led upward. In the late afternoon they did come to the top of the lower slopes and to the very foot of the mountains. The path they were following led them right up to the foot of an impassable precipice and there stopped dead.

Much-Afraid stood still and stared. The more she looked, the more stunned she felt. Then she began to tremble and shake all over, for the whole mountain range before her, as far as she could see to the left and right, rose up in unbroken walls of rock so high that it made her giddy when she put her head back and tried to look up to the top. The cliffs completely blocked the way before her, yet the path ran right up to them, then stopped. There was no sign of a track in any other direction, and there was no way at all by which the overhanging, terrifying wall of cliff could be ascended. They would have to turn back.

Just as this overwhelming realization came to her, Suffering caught her hand and pointed to the rocky walls. A hart, followed by a hind, had appeared from among the jumbled rocks around them and were now actually beginning to ascend the precipice.

As the three stood watching, Much-Afraid turned dizzy and faint, for she saw that the hart, which was leading the way, was following what appeared to be a narrow and intensely steep track which went zigzagging across the face of the cliff. In some parts it was only a narrow ledge, in others there appeared to be rough steps, but in certain places she saw that the track apparently broke right off.

Then the hart would leap across the gap and go

springing upward, always closely followed by the hind, who set her feet exactly where his had been, and leaped after him, as lightly, as sure-footed, and apparently unafraid as it was possible for any creature to be. So the two of them leaped and sprang with perfect grace and assurance up the face of the precipice and disappeared from sight over the top.

Much-Afraid covered her face with her hands and sank down on a rock with a horror and dread in her heart such as she had never felt before. Then she felt her two companions take her hands in theirs and heard them say, "Do not be afraid, Much-Afraid, this is not a dead end after all, and we shall not have to turn back. There is a way up the face of the precipice. The hart and the hind have shown it to us quite plainly. We shall be able to follow it too and make the ascent."

"Oh, no! No!" Much-Afraid almost shrieked. "That path is utterly impossible. The deer may be able to manage it, but no human being could. I could never get up there. I would fall headlong and be broken in pieces on those awful rocks." She burst into hysterical sobbing. "It's an impossibility, an absolute impossibility. I cannot get to the High Places that way, and so can never get there at all." Her two guides tried to say something more, but she put her hands over her ears and broke into another clamor of terrified sobs. There was the Shepherd's Much-Afraid, sitting at the foot of the precipice, wringing her hands and shaking with terror, sobbing over and over again, "I can't do it; I can't. I shall never get to the High Places." Nothing less like royalty could be imagined, but far worse was to follow.

As she crouched on the ground, completely exhausted, they heard a crunching sound and a rattling of loose stones, then a voice close beside her.

"Ha, ha! My dear little cousin, we meet again at last! How do you find yourself now, Much-Afraid, in this delightfully pleasant situation?"

She opened her eyes in fresh terror and found herself looking right into the hideous face of Craven Fear himself.

"I thought somehow," he went on with a look of the most horrible gloating. "Yes, I really thought that we could come together again at last. Did you really believe, you poor little fool, that you could escape from me altogether? No, no, Much-Afraid, you are one of the Fearings, and you can't evade the truth, and what is more, you trembling little idiot, you belong to me. I have come to take you back safely and make sure that you don't wander off again."

"I won't go with you," gasped Much-Afraid, too shocked by this awful apparition to have her wits about her. "I absolutely refuse to go with you."

"Well, you can take your choice," sneered Craven. "Take a look at the precipice before you, my dear cousin.

Won't you feel lovely up there! Just look where I'm pointing, Much-Afraid. See there, halfway up, where that dizzy little ledge breaks right off and you have to jump across the chasm on to that bit of rock. Just picture yourself jumping that, Much-Afraid, and finding yourself hanging over space, clutching a bit of slippery rock which you can't hold on to another minute. Just imagine those ugly, knife-like rocks at the foot of the precipice, waiting to receive and mangle you to pieces as your strength gives out, and you plunge down on them.

"Doesn't it give you a lovely feeling, Much-Afraid? Just take time to picture it. That's only one of many such broken places on the track, and the higher you go, you dear little fool, the farther you will have to fall. Well, take your choice. Either you must go up there, where you know that you can't, but will end in a mangled heap at the bottom, or you must come back and live with me and be my little slave ever afterward." And the rocks and cliffs seemed to echo again with his gloating laughter.

"Much-Afraid," said the two guides, stooping over her and shaking her by the shoulder gently but firmly. "Much-Afraid, you know where your help lies. Call for help."

She clung to them and sobbed again. "I am afraid to call," she gasped. "I am so afraid that if I call him, he will tell me that I must go that way, that dreadful, dreadful way, and I can't. It's impossible. I can't face it. Oh, what shall I do? Whatever shall I do?"

Sorrow bent over her and said very gently but urgently, "You must call for him, Much-Afraid. Call at once."

"If I call him," shuddered Much-Afraid through chattering teeth, "he will tell me to build an altar, and I can't. This time I can't."

Craven Fear laughed triumphantly and took a step toward her, but her two companions put themselves between him and his victim. Then Suffering looked at Sorrow, who nodded back. In answer to the nod Suffering took a small but very sharp knife which hung at her girdle, and bending over the crouching figure, pricked her. Much-Afraid cried out in anguish, and then, in utter despair at finding herself helpless in the presence of all three, did that which she ought to have done the moment the path brought them to the foot of the precipice. Though now she felt too ashamed to do it, she did so because she was forced by her extremity. She cried out, "O Lord, I am oppressed; undertake for me. My fears have taken hold upon me, and I am ashamed to look up."

"Why, Much-Afraid." It was the Shepherd's voice close beside her. "What is the matter? Be of good cheer, it is I, be not afraid."

He sounded so cheery and full of strength, and, moreover, without a hint of reproach, that Much-Afraid felt as though a strong and exhilarating cordial had been poured into her heart and that a stream of courage and strength was flowing into her from his presence.

She sat up and looked at him and saw that he was

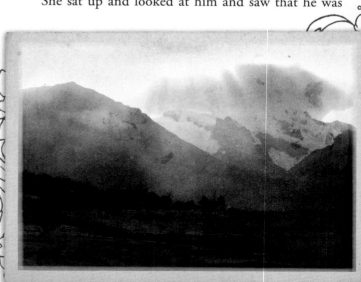

smiling, almost laughing at her. The shame in her eyes met no answering reproach in his, and suddenly she found words echoing in her heart which other trembling souls had spoken. "My Lord is of very tender compassion to them that are afraid." As she looked, thankfulness welled up in her heart and the icy hand of fear which had clutched her broke and melted away and joy burst into bloom. A little song ran through her mind like a trickling stream.

My Beloved is the chiefest
Of ten thousand anywhere.
He is altogether lovely
He is altogether fair,
My Beloved is so gentle
And is strong beyond compare.

"Much-Afraid," said the Shepherd again, "tell me, what is the matter. Why were you so fearful?"

"It is the way you have chosen for me to go," she whispered. "It looks so dreadful, Shepherd, so impossible. I turn giddy and faint whenever I look at it. The roes and hinds can go there, but they are not limping, crippled, or cowardly like me."

"But, Much-Afraid, what did I promise you in the Valley of Humiliation?" asked the Shepherd with a smile.

Much-Afraid looked startled, and the blood rushed into her cheeks and ebbed again, leaving them as white as before. "You said," she began and broke off and then began again. "O Shepherd, you said you would make my feet like hinds' feet and set me upon mine High Places."

"Well," he answered cheerily, "the only way to develop hinds' feet is to go by the paths which the hinds use—like this one."

Much-Afraid trembled and looked at him shamefacedly.

"I don't think—I want—hinds' feet, if it means I have to go on a path like that," she said slowly and painfully.

The Shepherd was a very surprising person. Instead of looking either disappointed or disapproving, he actually laughed again. "Oh, yes you do," he said cheerfully. "I know you better than you know yourself, Much-Afraid. You want it very much indeed, and I promise you these hinds' feet. Indeed, I have brought you on purpose to this back side of the desert, where the mountains are particularly steep and where there are no paths but the tracks of the deer and of the mountain goats for you to follow, that the promise may be fulfilled. What did I say to you the last time that we met?"

"You said, 'Now shalt thou see what I will do,'" she answered, and then, looking at him reproachfully, added, "But I never dreamed you would do anything like this! Lead me to an impassable precipice up which nothing can go but deer and goats, when I'm no more like a deer or a goat than is a jellyfish. It's too—it's too—" She fumbled for words, and then burst out laughing. "Why, it's too preposterously absurd! It's crazy! Whatever will you do next?"

The Shepherd laughed too. "I love doing preposterous things," he replied. "Why, I don't know anything more exhilarating and delightful than turning weakness into strength, and fear into faith, and that which has been marred into perfection. If there is one thing more than another which I should enjoy doing at this moment it is turning a jellyfish into a mountain goat. That is my special work," he added with the light of great joy in his face. "Transforming things—to take Much-Afraid, for instance and to transform her into—" He broke off and then went on laughingly. "Well, we shall see later on what she finds herself transformed into."

It was a really extraordinary scene. In the place where just a little while before all had been fear and despair were the Shepherd and Much-Afraid, sitting on the rocks at the foot of the impassable precipice, laughing together as though at the greatest joke in the world.

"Come now, little jellyfish," said the Shepherd, "do you believe that I can change you into a mountain goat and get you to the top of the precipice?"

"Yes," replied Much-Afraid.

"Will you let me do it?"

"Yes," she answered, "if you want to do such a crazy and preposterous thing, why certainly you may."

"Do you believe that I will let you be put to shame on the way up?"

Much-Afraid looked at him and then said something that she had never been willing to say before. "I don't think I mind so very much if you do; only have your will and way in me, Shepherd. Nothing else matters."

As she spoke, something lovely happened. A double rainbow appeared above the precipice, arching it completely, so that the zigzag path up which the roe and the doe had gone was framed in the glowing colors. It was such a beautiful and extraordinary sight

that Much-Afraid gasped with wonder and delight, but there was something else about it which was almost more wonderful. She saw that Sorrow and Suffering, who had drawn aside while the Shepherd spoke to her, were standing one at either side of the path, and where the ends of the rainbow touched the earth, one touched Suffering and the other Sorrow.

In the shining glory of the rainbow colors, the two veiled figures were so transfigured with beauty that Much-Afraid could only look at them for a moment before being dazzled.

Then she did that which only a short time before had seemed utterly impossible. She knelt down at the foot of the precipice and built an altar and laid on it her will, her dread, and her shrinking, and when the fire had fallen she found among the ashes a larger and rougher-looking stone than any of the others, sharp-edged and dark in color, but otherwise quite ordinary looking.

This she put in her purse and then rose to her feet and waited for the Shepherd to show her what to do. In her heart she was hoping that he would accompany her up the dreadful ascent as he had gone with her down into the desert, but this he did not do.

Instead, he led her to the foot of the precipice and said, "Now, Much-Afraid, you have really come at last to the foot of the High Places, and a new stage of the journey is to begin. There are new lessons for you to learn.

"I must tell you that this precipice to which the path has led you is at the foot of Mount Injury. The whole

MEMORIAL STONE Nº 6

mountain range stretches a long way beyond this in either direction, and everywhere it is as steep or even steeper than here. There are even more terrible precipices on the sides of Mount Reviling and Mount Hate and Mount Persecution and others besides, but nowhere is it possible to find a way up to the High Places and into the Kingdom of Love, without surmounting at least one of them. This is the one which I have chosen for you to ascend.

"On the way here you have been learning the lesson of acceptance-with-joy, which is the first letter in the alphabet of Love. Now you must learn the B of the alphabet of Love. You have come to the foot of Mount Injury, and I hope and expect that on the way up the precipice you will discover what is this next letter of the alphabet, and that you will learn and practice it as you have the A of Love. Remember that though you must now meet Injury and surmount it, there is nothing on the way up this terrible-looking precipice nor indeed anything that you may meet above and beyond it that can do you the slightest harm or hurt if you will learn and steadfastly practice the second lesson in the Ascent of Love."

When he had said this he put his hands upon her with special solemnity and gentleness and blessed her. Then he called her companions, who immediately stepped forward. Next he took a rope from a crevice in the wall of rock, and with his own hands roped together the three who were to ascend the precipice. Sorrow was in front and Suffering behind, with Much-Afraid in the middle, so that the two who were so strong and sure-footed went before and after.

In this way, even if Much-Afraid slipped and fell, they would be able to hold her up and support her by the rope.

Lastly, he put his hand to his side and brought out a little bottle of cordial which he gave to Much-Afraid, telling her to drink a little at once and to make use of it if ever she felt giddy or faint on the way up. The label on the bottle read, "Spirit of Grace and Comfort," and when Much-Afraid had taken a drop or two she felt so revived and strengthened that she was ready to begin the ascent without any feeling of faintness, although there was still a sensation of dread in her heart.

By this time the evening was well advanced, but being summer there were yet two or three hours before it would begin to be dark, and the Shepherd charged them to start at once for, said he, "Although you cannot possibly reach the top before nightfall, there is a cave farther up the cliff which you cannot see from here, and there you can rest and spend the night in perfect safety. If you stay down here at the foot of the precipice your enemies will most certainly steal up on you and seek to do you harm. However, they will not follow you up this track, and while you are going up you will be beyond their reach. Though I doubt not," he added warningly, "that you will meet them again when you have reached the top."

With that he smiled encouragingly up on them and immediately Sorrow put her foot upon the first step of the narrow little track which zigzagged up the face of the cliff. Much-Afraid followed next, and then Suffering, and in a moment or two they were beginning the ascent.

Ascent of the Precipice Injury

Once on the track, Much-Afraid discovered to her surprise and deep thankfulness that it was not nearly so appalling in actual fact as it had seemed in anticipation. Steep, difficult, and slippery it certainly was, and also painfully narrow, but the feeling of being securely roped to her strong companions was very reassuring. Also, the cordial of the Spirit of Grace and Comfort which she had just drunk kept her from feeling giddy and faint when she looked over the edge, the thing she had most dreaded. Moreover, for the first half-hour of their ascent the rainbow still shone above them, and though the Shepherd had disappeared from view Much-Afraid had a lovely sense that he was still close beside them.

She did not look down unless obliged to do so, but once quite soon after they had started she had to wait in a little niche in the rock at one of the difficult places while Sorrow felt her way forward and Suffering waited in the rear.

Just then, she looked down, and felt very thankful indeed that the Shepherd had charged them to start the ascent that evening and not spend the night down below. Sitting on the rocks below were all five of her enemies, gazing up at them and grimacing with fury and spite. Indeed, as she looked she was startled to see Self-Pity (who always looked less ugly and dangerous than his companions) stoop down and pick up a sharp stone which he flung at her with all his might. Fortunately they were already practically out of reach of stone-throwing, but the jagged piece did hit the cliff just below her, and Much-Afraid was greatly relieved when she felt Sorrow pull gently on the rope to tell her that she now could move forward.

She remembered the Shepherd's warning that she was likely to meet these enemies again when the precipice was surmounted though how they would get up onto the Mount Injury she did not know; only that there must be some other way which they could use.

So the three of them climbed higher and higher while the shadows thrown by the cliffs lengthened over the plain below and the sun went down in a blaze of glory beyond the desert and the great sea. From the height which they had now reached they could plainly see the western sea, along the shores of which they had traveled for so long.

The track they followed wound up and ever upward, back and forth across the face of the cliff, and though it was crumbling and even broken in some places, Much-Afraid was tremendously relieved to find that nowhere at all was it too difficult, not even at the spot halfway up the cliff which Craven Fear had so particularly pointed out to her.

On arriving there just as darkness fell, she found that though the path had indeed broken right away, a plank had been laid across the gap and a rope placed through iron rings in the rock face to form a handrail to which she could cling as she walked across the narrow bridge. The hart and the hind, of course, had disdained such unnecessary assistance and had leaped across the chasm, making it look as though there was nothing there. However, even with the handrail to steady her, Much-Afraid was very careful to close her imagination altogether to the picture which Craven Fear had painted. From bitter experience she knew that pictures thrown on the screen of her imagination could seem much more unnerving and terrible than the actual facts.

When the plank was crossed safely they discovered themselves to be in an exceedingly narrow gorge quite invisible from below. Directly facing them was the very resting place which the Shepherd had spoken of, a little cave where they were to pass the night.

With a sense of great relief and thankfulness she went inside and looked round. Its situation was such that though she could not look down into the dizzy depths beneath, it was possible to look right out over the plateau and the desert to the far-off sea. The moon had just risen and was shedding a pure silver light over everything, and the first stars appeared like faint flickers in the darkening sky. In the cave itself flat rocks had been placed to form rude seats and a table, and on the ground at one side were piled sheepskins on which they could rest.

Not far from the cave entrance a tiny waterfall trickled down the cliff, and they went to it in turn and refreshed themselves. Then Sorrow and Suffering produced two packages of bread and dried fruits and nuts which the Shepherd had given them at the foot of the ascent. With these they gladly satisfied their hunger, and then, overcome by weariness, they laid themselves down in the cave and fell into dreamless slumber.

Much-Afraid woke with the first light of dawn, and getting up, walked to the entrance of the cave. In the cold light of early morning she could not help telling herself that a scene of utter desolation lay before her. As far as the eye could see was nothing but empty plain and sea, with lowering cliffs above her and jagged rock below. The pleasant wooded country which they had left was out of sight, and in all the vast area upon which she looked she saw not a single tree and scarcely a stunted bush. "How desolate,"

Life can engulf us into unwanted chasms, and it is during these times that we must cling to the Good Shepherd. Reflect on a time when he miraculously presented a handrail to assist you across an unsteady bridge.

_____

_____

_____

thought Much-Afraid, "and those rocks beneath look very cruel indeed, as if they are waiting to injure and destroy anything which falls upon them. It seems as though nothing can grow anywhere in all this barren waste."

Just then she looked up at the cliffs above her head and started with surprise and delight. In a tiny crevice of the rock, where a few drops from the trickling waterfall could occasionally sprinkle it, was a single plant. It had just two or three leaves, and one fragile stem, almost hair-like in its slenderness, grew out at right angles to the wall. On the stem was one flower, blood red in color, which glowed like a lamp or flame of fire in the early rays of the sun.

Much-Afraid stared at it for some moments, noticing the wall which completely imprisoned it, the minute aperture through which it had forced its way to the light, and the barren loneliness of its surroundings. Its roots were clamped around by sheer rock, its leaves scarcely able to press outside the prison house, yet it had insisted on bursting into bloom, and was holding its little face open to the sun and burning like a flame of joy. As she looked up at it Much-Afraid asked, as she had in the desert, "What is your name, little flower, for indeed I never saw another like you."

At that moment the sun touched the blood-red petals so that they shone more vividly than ever, and a little whisper rustled from the leaves.

"My name is 'Bearing-the-Cost,' but some call me 'Forgiveness.'"

Then Much-Afraid recalled the words of the Shepherd,

"On the way up the precipice you will discover the next letter in the alphabet of Love. Begin to practice it at once."

She gazed at the little flower and said again, "Why call you that?"

Once more, a little whispering laugh passed through the leaves, and she thought she heard them say, "I was separated from all my companions, exiled from home, carried here and imprisoned in this rock. It was not my choice, but the work of others who, when they had dropped me here, went away and left me to bear the results of what they had done. "I have borne and have not fainted; I have not ceased to love, and Love helped me push through the crack in the rock until I could look right out onto my Love the sun himself. See now! There is nothing whatever between my Love and my heart, nothing around to distract me from him. He shines upon me and makes me to rejoice, and has atoned to me for all that was taken from me and done against me. There is no flower in all the world more blessed or more satisfied than I, for I look up to him as a weaned child and say, 'Whom have I in heaven but thee, and there is none upon earth that I desire but thee.'"

Much-Afraid looked at the glowing flame above her head, and a longing which was almost envy leaped into her heart. She knew what she must do. Kneeling on the narrow path beneath the imprisoned flower, she said, "O my Lord, behold me—I am thy little handmaiden Bearing-the-Cost."

At that moment a fragment of the rock which imprisoned the roots of the flower above her loosened and fell at her feet. She picked it up and put it very gently with the other seven stones in her purse, then returned to the cave. Sorrow and Suffering were waiting for her with a further supply of bread and raisins and nuts, and after they had given thanks and had eaten, they roped themselves together again and continued up the precipice.

After a little they came to a place which was very steep and slippery. Suddenly Much-Afraid had her first fall and cut herself quite badly on the pieces of jagged rock which had tripped her. It was a good thing she was so securely roped, for a great terror came upon her and she became so giddy and faint that had she not been tied she might have slipped over the edge of the path and been dashed to pieces on the rocks below. As this thought struck her she was so overcome with panic and trembling that all she could do was to crouch against the wall of rock and cry out to her companions that she was fainting and was in terror of falling.

Immediately Sorrow, who was in front, tightened the rope, then Suffering came up to her, put her arms around her and said urgently, "Drink some of the cordial which the Shepherd gave you."

Much-Afraid was so faint and frightened that she could only lie in the arms of Suffering and gasp, "I don't know where the bottle is—I can't move even to fumble for it."

Then Suffering herself put her hand into the bosom of the fainting girl, drew out the bottle, and poured a few drops between her lips. After a few moments the color returned to Much-Afraid's cheeks, and the faintness

 MEMORIAL STONE № 7

began to pass off, but still she could not move. She took more of the Spirit of Grace and Comfort and began to feel strengthened.

Then Sorrow, who had come back to the place where she was crouching, gently shortened the rope so that Much-Afraid could take her hand and again they started to climb. In the fall, however, Much-Afraid had cut both knees so severely that she could only limp forward very painfully, moaning continually and halting constantly. Her companions were very patient, but progress was so slow that finally it became necessary to make greater speed, or they would not reach the top of the precipice before nightfall, and there was no other cave where they could rest.

At last Suffering stooped over her and asked, "Much-Afraid, what were you doing when you left the cave this morning and went off by yourself?"

Much-Afraid gave her a startled look, then said with a painful flush, "I was looking at a flower which I had not seen before, growing in the rock by the waterfall."

"What flower was that?" persisted Suffering very gently.

"It was the flower of Bearing-the-Cost," replied

Much-Afraid in a very low voice, "but some call it Forgiveness." For a few moments she was silent, remembering the altar she had built and realizing that she was not practicing this new and difficult letter of the Alphabet of Love. Then said she, "I wonder if it would help my knees if we put a few drops of the cordial on them."

"Let us try," said Sorrow and Suffering both together. "It is an excellent suggestion."

As they dropped a little of the cordial on both knees, almost at once the bleeding ceased, and the worst of the smart and pain died away. Her legs remained very stiff and she was still obliged to limp quite badly, but they did go forward at a much better pace. By late afternoon they were right at the top of the awful ascent, and found themselves in a forest of young pine trees with moss and blueberries growing on the banks beside the path, and the precipice which had looked so impassable actually behind them. They sat down on one of the mossy banks in the wood to rest, then heard a voice singing quite close at hand.

Thou art all fair, my dearest love,
There is no spot in thee.
Come with me to the heights above,
Yet fairer visions see.
Up to the mount of Myrrh and thence
Across the hills of Frankincense,
To where the dawn's clear innocence
Bids all the shadows flee.
Come with me, O my fairest dear,
With me to Lebanon,
Look from the peaks of grim Shenir,
Amana and Hermon.
The lions have their dens up there—
The leopards prowl the glens up there,
But from the top the view is clear
Of land yet to be won.

CANT. 4:7-8

There, coming toward them through a clearing in the trees, was the Shepherd himself.

In the Forests of Danger and Tribulation

With what joy they welcomed the Shepherd as he sat down in their midst, and after cheerfully congratulating them on having surmounted the precipice, he laid his hands gently on the wounds which Much-Afraid had received when she fell, and immediately they were healed. Then he began to speak to them about the way which lay ahead.

"You have now to go through the forests which clothe the sides of these mountains almost up to the snowline. The way will be steep, but you will come to resting places here and there. These are the Forests of Danger and Tribulation, and often the pine trees grow so tall and so closely together that the path may seem quite dark. Storms are very frequent up here on these slopes, but keep pressing forward, for remember that nothing can do you any real harm while you are following the path of my will."

It did seem strange that even after safely surmounting so many difficulties and steep places, including the "impassable precipice" just below them, Much-Afraid should remain so like her name. But so it was! No sooner did the Shepherd pronounce the words "danger and tribulation" than she began to shake and tremble all over again.

"The Forests of Danger and Tribulation!" she repeated with a piteous quaver in her voice. "O Shepherd, wherever will you lead me next?"

"To the next stage on the way to the High Places," he answered promptly, smiling at her as nicely as possible.

"I wonder if you will ever be able to get me there!" groaned poor foolish little Much-Afraid. "I wonder you continue to bother with me and don't give up the job altogether. It looks as though I never shall have anything but lame feet, and that even you won't be able to make them

YEA, THOUGH I WALK THROUGH THE VALLEY OF THE SHADOW OF DEATH, I WILL FEAR NO EVIL: FOR THOU ART WITH ME.

PSALM 23:4

like hinds' feet." She looked disconsolately at her feet as she spoke. Certainly at the moment they did look even more crooked than ever.

"I am not a man that I should lie," said the Shepherd gravely. "Look at me, Much-Afraid. Do you believe that I will deceive you? Have I said, and shall I not do it? Or have I spoken, and shall I not make it good?"

Much-Afraid trembled a little, partly at the tone of his voice and partly because she was still Much-Afraid by nature and was already trying to picture what the Forests of Danger and Tribulation would be like. That always had a disastrous effect upon her, but she answered penitently, "No—I know that you are not a man who would lie to me; I know that you will make good what you have said."

"Then," said the Shepherd, speaking very gently again, "I am going to lead you through danger and tribulation, Much-Afraid, but you need not be the least bit afraid, for I shall be with you. Even if I lead you through the Valley of the Shadow itself you need not fear, for my rod and my staff will comfort you."

Then he added, "Thou shalt not be afraid for the terror by night; nor for the arrow that flieth by day; nor for the pestilence that walketh in darkness; nor for the destruction that wasteth at noonday. Though a thousand fall at thy side, and ten thousand at thy right hand, it shall not come nigh thee. . . . For I will cover thee with my feathers and under my wings shalt thou trust" (Psa. 91:4-7). The gentleness of his voice as he said these things was indescribable.

Then Much-Afraid knelt at his feet and built yet another altar and said, "Yea, though I walk through the Valley of the Shadow of Death, I will fear no evil; for thou art with me." Then, because she found that even as she spoke her teeth were chattering with fright and her hands

had gone quite clammy, she looked up into his face and added, "For thou art not a man that thou shouldest lie, nor the Son of man that thou shouldest repent. Hast thou said, and shalt thou not do it? And hast thou spoken and shalt thou not make it good?"

Then the Shepherd smiled more comfortingly than ever before, laid both hands on her head and said, "Be strong, yea, be strong and fear not." Then he continued, "Much-Afraid, don't ever allow yourself to begin trying to picture what it will be like. Believe me, when you get to the places which you dread you will find that they are as different as possible from what you have imagined, just as was the case when you were actually ascending the precipice. I must warn you that I see your enemies lurking among the trees ahead, and if you ever let Craven Fear begin painting a picture on the screen of your imagination, you will walk with fear and trembling and agony, where no fear is."

When he had said this, he picked up another stone from the place where she was kneeling, and gave it to her to put with the other memorial stones. Then he went his way, and Much-Afraid and her companions started on the path which led up through the forests.

Almost as soon as they had reached the trees they saw the face of mean, sickly Self-Pity, looking out from behind one of the trunks. He gabbled ever so quickly before he dodged back into hiding, "I say, Much-Afraid, this really is a bit too thick. I mean, whatever will he do next, forcing

 MEMORIAL STONE № 8

_____

_____

_____

a poor little lame, frightened creature like yourself to go through dangers which only brave, strong men ought to be expected to face. Really, your Shepherd is almost more of a bully than Craven Fear himself."

Hardly had he stopped before Resentment put his head out and said crossly, "There's absolutely no reason for it either, because there's another perfectly good path which skirts the forest altogether and brings you right up to the snowline without going anywhere near these unnecessary dangers. Everybody else goes that way, so why shouldn't you? Tell him you won't go this way, Much-Afraid, and insist on being taken by the usual path. This way is for martyrs only, and you, my dear, don't fit into the picture at all."

Then Craven Fear leered at her for a moment and said contemptuously, "So you think you're going to become a little heroine, do you? and go singing through the Forest of Danger! What will you bet, Much-Afraid, that you won't end up shrieking and screaming like a maniac, maimed for the rest of your life?"

Bitterness was next to speak, and sneered from behind another tree, "He would do this. It's just as I told you. After you have dutifully gone through one terrifying experience he's always got something still worse lying ahead of you."

Then Pride (who was still limping badly and seemed extra venomous as a result) said, "You know, he won't be able to rest content until he has put you to complete shame, because that's the way he produces that precious humility he's so crazy about. He'll humble you to the dust, Much-Afraid, and leave you a groveling idiot in front of everyone."

Much-Afraid and her companions walked on without answering and without taking any notice, but as before,

Much-Afraid discovered that she limped more painfully whenever she heard what they said. It was really terribly perplexing to know what to do. If she listened, she limped, and if she put her fingers in her ears, she couldn't accept the hands of her two guides, which meant that she stumbled and slipped.

So they stopped for a moment or two and discussed the matter, and then Suffering opened the little First Aid kit hanging at her girdle, took out some cotton and firmly plugged the ears of Much-Afraid. Although this was uncomfortable, it did seem to have the desired effect, at least temporarily, for when the five sulkers saw that they could not make her hear them they soon tired of bawling at her and left her alone until another opportunity should occur for badgering her again.

At first the forest did not really seem too dreadful. Perhaps it was that up there on the mountains the air was so fresh and strong that it made those who breathed it fresh and strong too. Also, the sun was still shining, and Much-Afraid began to feel a sensation which was completely new to her, a thrill of excitement and, incredible as it seemed, of almost pleasurable adventure.

Here she was, lame Much-Afraid, actually walking through the Forest of Danger and not really minding. This lasted for quite a time until huge black clouds gradually rolled over the sky, and the sun went in. In the distance thunder rolled and the woods became dark and very still. Suddenly a bolt of lightning scorched across the sky, and somewhat ahead of them was a rending crash as a great forest tree fell to the earth, then another and another. Then the storm in all its fury was bursting around them, thunder rolling, lightning sizzling and crackling in every direction until the whole forest seemed to be groaning and shaking and falling about them.

The strangest thing was that though Much-Afraid felt a shuddering thrill go through her at every crash she was not really afraid. That is, she felt neither panic nor desire to run, nor even real dread, for she kept repeating to herself, "Though a thousand shall fall at thy side and ten thousand at thy right hand, it shall not come nigh thee. . . . For I will cover thee with my feathers, and under my wings shalt thou trust." So throughout the whole storm she was filled with a strange and wonderful peace such as she had never felt before, and walked between her two companions saying to herself, "I shall not die, but live and declare the works of the Lord."

At last the storm began to rumble off into the distance, the crashes died down, and there was a quiet lull. The three women stopped to wring the water out of their clothes and hair and try to tidy themselves. As they did this, Craven Fear appeared near them again and yelled at the top of his voice, "I say, Much-Afraid, the storm has only gone round the mountains for a short time. Already it is beginning to approach again and will be worse than before. Make a bolt back down the path as quickly as you can and get away from these dangerous trees before it starts again or you will be killed. There is just time for you to make good your escape."

"Look here," exclaimed Much-Afraid most unexpectedly, water still dripping from her hair and her sodden skirts clinging like wet rags around her legs, "I can't stand that fellow shouting at me any longer. Please help me—both of you," and setting the example, she stooped down, picked up a stone and flung it straight at Craven Fear.

Her two companions actually laughed for the very first time and started hurling a barrage of stones among the trees where the five were lurking. In a moment or two none of their enemies were visible. Then, just ahead of them,

through the trees, they saw a log hut which seemed to offer a promise of shelter and protection from the storm, which certainly was again drawing nearer. Hurrying toward the cabin, they found that it stood in a clearing well away from the trees, and when they tried the door latch, to their joy it opened and they thankfully slipped inside. With great presence of mind, Suffering immediately closed the door and bolted it behind them, and none too soon!

Next minute their enemies were banging on the door and shouting, "Hi! I say—open the door and let us in. The storm is starting again. You can't be so inhuman as to shut us outside and leave us to our fate."

Much-Afraid went to the door and shouted through the keyhole the advice they had offered her, "Make a bolt down the path as quickly as you can and get away from these dangerous trees, or you will be killed. You have just time to make good your escape before the storm starts again."

There was a sound of muttered curses outside, then of hurrying feet fading away into the distance, and it seemed as though this time the advice was being acted upon. Back rolled the storm, fiercer and more terrible than before, but they were safely sheltered in the hut out of range of the crashing trees, and their shelter proved perfectly weatherproof, for not a drop came through the roof.

They found in the room a supply of firewood stacked beside a small kitchen range with a kettle and some saucepans on it. While Suffering busied herself lighting the fire, Sorrow held the kettle under a spout outside the window and filled it with rain water. Much-Afraid went to a cupboard on the wall to see if it would yield any treasure. Sure enough, there was crockery on the shelves and a supply of tinned foods, as well as a big tin of unleavened biscuits.

So in a very little time, while the storm still furiously raged and rattled outside, there they were, sitting around a crackling fire, warming themselves and drying their sopping garments while they drank comforting hot cocoa and satisfied their hunger. Though the uproar of the tempest without was almost deafening and the hut shuddered and shook in every blast, yet inside was nothing but peace and thanksgiving and cheerful contentment.

Much-Afraid found herself thinking with astonished awe that it was really the happiest and the most peaceful experience during the whole of her journey up till that time. As they lay down on the mattresses which they discovered piled in another part of the hut, she repeated again to herself very softly: "He has covered me with his feathers, and under his wings I do trust."

The storm continued with great violence for two or three days, but while it lasted the three travelers rested quietly in the shelter of the hut, going outside only during the brief lulls to gather wood. This they dried in the oven to replenish the stock they were using, so that others, following on behind, might not be left without fuel. There seemed to be a good store of tinned foods and unleavened biscuits and they supposed that some of the Shepherd's servants must visit the hut from time to time with a new supply.

During those quiet days in the midst of the raging tempest Much-Afraid came to know her two companions in a new way and also to understand more of the mountain dialect which they spoke. In some strange way she began to feel that they were becoming real friends, and not just attendants whom the Shepherd had commanded to go with her as guides and helpers. She found, too, that now she was accepting their companionship in this way she seemed more alive than ever before to beauty and delight in the world around her.

It seemed as though her senses had been quickened in some extraordinary way, enabling her to enjoy every little detail of her life; so that although her companions actually were Sorrow and Suffering, she often felt an almost inexplicable joy and pleasure at the same time. This would happen when she looked at the bright, crackling flames in the log fire, or listened to the sound of lashing rain overhead emphasizing the safety and peace within the hut, or when she saw through the window the tossing trees waving their arms against a background of scurrying clouds or lightning-rent sky. Or again, very early before daybreak, when she saw the morning star shining serenely through a rift in the clouds or heard the clear, jubilant note of a bird during a lull in the storm.

All these things seemed to be speaking to her in the mountain dialect, and to her growing astonishment, she found it an incredibly beautiful language, so that sometimes her eyes filled with tears of pure joy and her heart seemed so full of ecstasy that she could hardly bear it.

One morning when the storm was rattling and raging through the forest louder than ever, she noticed Sorrow sitting by the fire singing quietly to herself, the words, of course, being in the mountain dialect, which Much-Afraid was learning to understand. This is the best translation that I can give, but you will realize that the original was much more beautiful and full of forest sounds and music.

How lovely and how nimble are thy feet,
O prince's daughter!
They flash and sparkle
And can run more fleet
Than running water.
On all the mountains there is no gazelle,
No roe or hind,
Can overtake thee nor can leap as well—
But lag behind.

CANT. 7:1

"Why, Sorrow," exclaimed Much-Afraid, "I didn't know that you could sing, nor even that you knew any songs."

Sorrow answered quietly, "Neither did I, but on the way up here through the forest I found the words and tune coming into my head just as I am singing them now."

"I like it," said Much-Afraid. "It makes me think of the time when I shall have hinds' feet myself, and so it is comforting and the tune is so nice and springy. It makes me want to jump." She laughed at the thought of her crooked feet being able to jump, then coaxed, "Teach me the song—please do."

So Sorrow sang it over several times until Much-Afraid knew it perfectly and went about the hut humming it to herself, trying to picture what it would be like to be a gazelle leaping on the mountains, and able to jump from crag to crag, just as the Shepherd did. When the day came for her to receive her hinds' feet, she would be able to follow him wherever he went. The picture was so lovely she could hardly wait for it to come true.

In the Mist

AT LAST THE STORM gradually died down, the clamor on the mountains ceased, and it was time to resume the journey. However, the weather had broken completely, and though the storm itself was over, thick mist and cloud remained, shrouding everything on the heights.

When they started the mist was so thick that they could see only the trees on either side of the narrow path, and even they looked ghostly and unreal. The rest of the forest was simply swallowed up and entirely lost to sight, veiled in a cold and clammy white curtain. The ground was dreadfully muddy and slippery, and although the path did not climb nearly so steeply as before, after some hours Much-Afraid found to her amazement that she was missing the rolling thunder of the storm and even the sickening crash of the trees as the lightning splintered them.

She began to realize that, cowardly though she was, there was something in her which responded with a surge of excitement to the tests and difficulties of the way better than to easier and duller circumstances. It was true that fear sent a dreadful shuddering thrill through her, but nevertheless it was a thrill, and she found herself realizing with astonishment that even the dizzy precipice had been more to her liking than this dreary plodding on and on through the bewildering mist. In some way the dangers of the storm had stimulated her; now there was nothing but tameness, just a trudge, trudge forward, day after day, able to see nothing except for white, clinging mist which hung about the mountains without a gleam of sunshine breaking through.

At last she burst out impatiently, "Will this dull, dreary mist never lift, I wonder?" And would you believe it! A voice she knew all too well immediately answered from beyond the trees.

"No, it won't," replied Resentment. "Moreover you might just as well know now that this is going to continue for no one knows how long. Higher up the mountains the mist hangs thicker and thicker still. That's all you can expect for the rest of the Journey."

Much-Afraid pretended not to hear, but the voice went on again almost at once.

"Have you noticed, Much-Afraid, that the path which you are following isn't going up the mountain at all, but is almost level? You've missed the upward way, and you are just going round and round the mountain in circles."

Much-Afraid had not exactly noticed this fact, but now she could not help realizing that it was true. They were not climbing at all, but simply moving along the mountainside with constant ups and downs, and the downs seemed to be getting more frequent. Could it be possible that they were really gradually descending the mountain instead of going up? In the bewildering mist one simply could not see anything, and she found she had lost all sense of direction. On asking her companions what they thought about it they answered rather shortly (because, of course, she ought not to have listened to any suggestion from Resentment) that they were on the path which the Shepherd had pointed out, and would certainly not allow anyone to persuade them to leave it.

"But," persisted Much-Afraid petulantly, "don't you think that we may have missed the way in this mist? The Shepherd said the path led upward, and as you see, this one doesn't. It runs along the side of the mountain. There may easily have been a more direct way up which we didn't notice in the mist."

Their only answer was that they knew better than to listen to any suggestion made by Resentment.

At that the voice of Bitterness broke in quite clearly, "You might at least be willing to go back a little way and look, instead of insisting on going on and on along what may prove to be a wrong path leading you round in circles."

Sorrow and Suffering took absolutely no notice, but unfortunately Much-Afraid did, and said with still greater petulance, "I think you ought to consider the suggestion. Perhaps it would be better to go back a little way and see if we have missed the right path. Really, it is no use going on and on in circles, getting nowhere."

To this they replied, "Well, if we are going round in circles, we shall eventually arrive back where we went wrong, and if we keep our eyes open we shall be able to see the path we missed—always provided that it does exist and is not just a bit of imagination on the part of Bitterness."

"You poor little thing," came the whisper of Self-Pity through the mist. "It is too bad that you have been put in the charge of such obstinate mule-like creatures. Just think of the time you are wasting, getting nowhere at all. Trudge, trudge, day after day, nothing to show for it, and you ought to be getting up onto the High Places."

So they went on, whispering and talking at her through the clinging mist, which shrouded everything and made it all seem so ghostly and dreary. Of course, she ought not to have listened to them, but the mist was so bewildering and the path so unspeakably tame that she found something in her heart responding to them almost against her will.

Suffering doggedly led the way, and Sorrow just as

doggedly was her rearguard, so that there was no possibility of turning back, but Much-Afraid found herself limping and slipping and stumbling far more often and badly than at any other stage of the journey. It made her very disagreeable and difficult to deal with. It is true that after every stumble her conscience smote her and she apologized sorrowfully and abjectly to her companions, but that did not prevent her slipping again almost directly afterwards. Altogether it was a miserable time, and the mist, instead of clearing, seemed to get thicker and colder and drearier than ever.

At last, one afternoon, when the only word which at all described her progress is to say that she was slithering along the path, all muddy and wet and bedraggled from constant slips, she decided to sing.

It has not been mentioned before, but Much-Afraid did not possess the gift of sweet voice any more than a pretty face. It is true that she was fond of singing and that if the Shepherd sang with her she could keep in tune and manage quite nicely, but if she tried alone the results were by no means so good. However, the mist was so thick and clammy that she was nearly stifled, and she felt she must do something to try to cheer herself and to drown the ghostly voices which kept whispering to her through the trees.

It was not pleasant to think of her relatives now having the opportunity to entertain themselves at the expense of her very unmelodious voice, but she decided to risk their ribald comments. "If I sing quite loudly," she told herself, "I shall not be able to hear what they say." The only song which she could think of at the moment was the one which Sorrow had taught her in the hut, and though it seemed singularly inappropriate she lifted up her voice and sang quaveringly:

How lovely and how nimble are thy feet,
O prince's daughter!
They flash and sparkle
And can run more fleet
Than running water.
On all the mountains there is no gazelle,
No roe or hind,
Can overtake thee nor can leap as well—
But lag behind.

CANT. 7:1

There was perfect silence as she sang. The loud, sneering voices of her enemies had died away altogether. "It is a good idea," said Much-Afraid to herself jubilantly. "I wish I had thought of it before. It is a much better way to avoid hearing what they are saying than putting cotton in my ears, and I believe, yes, I really do believe, there is a little rift in the mist ahead. How lovely, I shall sing the verse again." And she did so.

"Why, Much-Afraid," said a cheery voice close beside her, "I have not heard that song before. Where did you learn it?"

There, striding toward her with a particularly pleased smile on his face, was the Shepherd himself. It is just impossible to describe in words the joy of Much-Afraid when she saw him really coming toward them on that dreary mountain path, where everything had been swallowed up for so long in the horrible mist and everything one touched had been so cold and clammy. Now with his coming the mist was rapidly clearing away and a real gleam of sunshine—the first they had seen for days—broke through at last.

"O Shepherd," she gasped, and caught hold of his hand and could say no more. It really had seemed as though she would never see him again.

"Tell me," he repeated cheerily as he smiled at them all, "where did you learn that song, Much-Afraid?"

"Sorrow taught it to me," she replied. "I didn't think that she knew any songs, Shepherd, but she said the words and the music came to her as we were climbing up through the forest. I asked her to teach it to me because—I know I am a goose, but it makes me think of the time when you will have made my feet like hinds' feet and I won't ever have to slither along again," and she looked shamefacedly at her bedraggled and muddy condition.

"I am glad you sing it," said the Shepherd more pleasantly than ever. "I think it is a particularly nice song. Indeed," he added smiling, "I think I will add another verse to it myself," and at once he began to sing these words to the same tune:

Thy joints and thighs are like a supple band
On which are met
Fair jewels which a cunning master hand
Hath fitly set.
In all the palace, search where'er you please,
In every place
There's none that walks with such a
Queenly ease,
Nor with just grace.

CANT. 7:1

"O Shepherd," exclaimed Much-Afraid, "where did you find that verse to fit in so nicely to the tune which Sorrow taught me?"

Again he smiled at her in the nicest possible way and answered, "The words came to me just now as I followed you along the path."

Poor Much-Afraid, who knew that she had been slipping and stumbling in the most dreadful way, indeed worse than at any other time, flushed painfully all over her face. She said nothing, only looked at him almost reproachfully.

"Much-Afraid," said he very gently in answer to that look, "don't you know by now that I never think of you as you are now but as you will be when I have brought you to the Kingdom of Love and washed you from all the stains and defilements of the journey? If I come along behind you and notice that you are finding the way especially difficult, and are suffering from slips and falls, it only makes me think of what you will be like when you are with me, leaping and skipping on the High Places. Wouldn't you like to learn and sing my verse just as much as the one which Sorrow taught you?"

"Yes," said Much-Afraid thankfully, and taking his hand again, "certainly I will learn it and sing about the cunning master hand which takes such pains with me."

By this time the mist had actually melted right away and the sun, shining brilliantly, was making the dripping trees and grass sparkle with joy and brightness. All three thankfully accepted the suggestion of the Shepherd that they should sit down for a short time and rest and rejoice in the sunshine. Sorrow and Suffering withdrew a little, as they always did when the Shepherd was present, leaving him to talk with Much-Afraid alone. She told him all the dismal tale of their long wanderings in the mist, the way Resentment, Bitterness, and Self-Pity had been bothering her and her fear that perhaps, after all, they had wandered from the path and lost their way.

"Did you really think that I would let you stray from the right path to the High Places without doing anything to warn you or to prevent it?" asked the Shepherd quietly.

She looked at him sorrowfully and said with a sigh, "When Resentment and the others are shouting at me

Take a moment to reflect on a time when you aimlessly wândered
through the mist, slipping and falling down life's path. In what
ways did you sense the Good Shepherd following behind you, allowing
you to stumble in order to prepare you for the High Places?

_____

_____

_____

_____

I am almost ready to believe anything, no matter how preposterous."

"You had better become a singer," said he, smiling. "Then you won't hear what they say to you. Ask Sorrow and Suffering if they have any more songs which they can teach you. Do you find them good guides, Much-Afraid?"

She looked at him earnestly and nodded her head. "Yes, very good. I never could have believed it possible, Shepherd, but in a way, I have come to love them. When I first saw them they looked so terrifyingly strong and stern, and I was sure that they would be rough with me and just drag me along without caring how I felt. How I dreaded it, but they have dealt with me very, very kindly indeed. I think they must have learned to be so gentle and patient with me by seeing your gentleness.

"I never could have managed without them," she went on gratefully,

"and the queer thing is I have a feeling that they really like helping an ugly little cripple like me in this way. They do truly want to get me up to the High Places, not just because it is the commandment which you have given them, but also because they want a horrid coward like myself to get there and be changed. You know, Shepherd, it makes a great difference in my feelings toward them not to look upon them any longer with dread, but as friends who want to help me. I know it seems ridiculous, but sometimes I get the feeling that they really love me and want to go with me of their own free will."

As she finished speaking she looked up in his face and was surprised to see that he actually looked as though he were trying not to laugh. He said nothing for a moment or two, but turned slightly so that he could look round at the two guides. Much-Afraid looked too.

They were sitting apart in the background and were unaware that they were being watched. They sat close to one another and were looking away up to the mountains toward the High Places. Their veils had been thrown back, although she still could not see their faces because their backs were toward the Shepherd and herself. She was struck by the fact that they seemed even taller and stronger than when she had first seen them waiting for her at the foot of the mountains.

There was something almost indescribably majestic about them at that moment, a sort of radiant eagerness expressed in their attitude. They were talking quickly to one another, but their voices were so low that she could not catch what they were saying. Was it possible—yes it was! They were actually laughing! That they were talking about something which thrilled them with eagerness and expectation, she felt quite sure.

The Shepherd watched them for a few moments

without speaking, then he turned back to Much-Afraid. His eyes were laughing at her, but he said quite gravely, "Yes, I really believe you are right, Much-Afraid. They do look to me as though they really enjoy their task, and perhaps even feel a little affection for the one they serve." Then he really did laugh out loud.

Sorrow and Suffering dropped the veils back over their faces and looked round to see what was happening, but the Shepherd had something more to say before he sped them farther on the journey.

The laughter died out on his face, and very seriously he asked, "Do you love me enough to be able to trust me completely, Much-Afraid?"

She looked at him in the usual startled fashion so natural to her whenever she sensed that he was preparing her for a new test, then faltered, "You know that I do love you, Shepherd, as much as my cold little heart is capable. You know that I love you and that I long to trust you as much as I love you, that I long both to love and trust you still more."

"Would you be willing to trust me," he asked, "even if everything in the wide world seemed to say that I was deceiving you—indeed, that I had deceived you all along?"

She looked at him in perplexed amazement. "Why, yes," she said, "I'm sure I would, because one thing I know to be true, it is impossible that you should tell a lie. It is impossible that you should deceive me. I know that I am often very frightened at the things which you ask me to do," she added shamefacedly and apologetically, "but I could never doubt you in that way. It's myself I am afraid of, never of you, and though everyone in the world should tell me that you had deceived me, I should know it was impossible.

"O Shepherd," she implored, "Don't tell me that you

think I really doubt you, even when I am most afraid and cowardly and despicably weak. You know—you know I trust you. In the end I know I shall be able to say thy gentleness hath made me great."

He said nothing for a little, only looked down very tenderly, almost pitifully at the figure now crouching at his feet. Then after a time, he said very quietly, "Much-Afraid, supposing I really did deceive you? What then?"

It was then her turn to be quite silent, trying to grasp this impossible thing he was suggesting and to think what her answer would be. What then? Would it be that she could never trust, never love him again? Would she have to be alive in the world where there was no Shepherd, only a mirage and broken lovely dream? To know that she had been deceived by one she was certain could not deceive? To lose him?

Suddenly she burst into a passion of weeping, then after a little while looked straight up into his face and said, "My Lord—if you can deceive me, you may. It can make no difference. I must love you as long as I continue to exist. I cannot live without loving you."

He laid his hands on her head, then with a touch more tender and gentle than anything she had ever felt before, repeated as though to himself, "If I can, I may deceive her." Then without another word he turned and went away.

Much-Afraid picked up a little icy-cold pebble which was lying on the ground where he had stood, put it in her bag, then tremblingly rejoined Sorrow and Suffering, and they continued their journey.

 MEMORIAL STONE № 9

_____

_____

_____

In the Valley of Loss

THE MIST HAD CLEARED from the mountains and the sun was shining, and as a consequence the way seemed much more pleasant and easy than it had for a very long time. The path still led them along the side of the mountain rather than upward, but one day, on turning a corner, they found themselves looking down into a deep valley. To their surprise, their path actually plunged straight down the mountainside toward it, exactly as at the beginning of the journey when Much-Afraid had been led down into Egypt.

All three halted and looked first at one another, then down into the valley and across to the other side. There the ascent was as steep and even higher than the Precipice of Injury and they saw that to go down and then ascend again would not only require an immense amount of strength and effort, but also take a very long time.

Much-Afraid stood and stared, and at that moment experienced the sharpest and keenest test which she had yet encountered on the journey. Was she to be turned aside once again, but in an even more terrible way than ever before? By now they had ascended far higher than ever before. Indeed, if only the path they were following would begin to ascend, they could not doubt that they would soon be at the snowline and approaching the real High Places, where no enemies could follow and where the healing streams flowed.

Now instead of that the path was leading them down into a valley as low as the Valley of Humiliation itself. All the height which they had gained after their long and toilsome journey must now be lost and they would have to begin all over again, just as though they had never made a start so long ago and endured so many difficulties and tests.

As she looked down into the depths of the valley the heart of Much-Afraid went numb. For the first time on the journey she actually asked herself if her relatives had not been right after all and if she ought not to have attempted to follow the Shepherd. How could one follow a person who asked so much, who demanded such impossible things, who took away everything? If she went down there, as far as getting to the High Places was concerned she must lose everything she had gained on the journey so far. She would be no nearer receiving the promise than when she started out from the Valley of Humiliation.

For one black, awful moment Much-Afraid really considered the possibility of following the Shepherd no longer, of turning back. She need not go on. There was absolutely no compulsion about it. She had been following this strange path with her two companions as guides simply because it was the Shepherd's choice for her. It was not the way which she naturally wanted to go. Now she could make her own choice. Her sorrow and suffering could be ended at once, and she could plan her life in the way she liked best, without the Shepherd.

During that awful moment or two it seemed to Much-Afraid that she was actually looking into an abyss of horror, into an existence in which there was no Shepherd to follow or to trust or to love—no Shepherd at all, nothing but her own horrible self. Ever after, it seemed that she had looked straight down into Hell. At the end of that moment Much-Afraid shrieked—there is no other word for it.

"Shepherd," she shrieked, "Shepherd! Shepherd! Help me! Where are you? Don't leave me!" Next instant she was clinging to him, trembling from head to foot, and sobbing over and over again, "You may do anything, Shepherd. You may ask anything—only don't let me turn back. O my Lord, don't let me leave you. Entreat me not to leave thee nor to return from following after thee." Then as she continued to cling to him she sobbed out, "If you can deceive me, my Lord, about the promise and the hinds' feet and the new name or anything else, you may, indeed you may; only don't let me leave you. Don't let anything turn me back. This path looked so wrong I could hardly believe it was the right one," and she sobbed bitterly.

He lifted her up, supported her by his arm, and with his own hand wiped the tears from her cheeks, then said in his strong cheery voice, "there is no question of your turning back, Much-Afraid. No one, not even your own shrinking heart, can pluck you out of my hand. Don't you remember what I told you before? 'This delay is not unto death but for the glory of God.' You haven't forgotten already the lesson you have been learning, have you?

"It is no less true now that 'what I do thou knowest not now, but thou shalt know hereafter.' My sheep hear my voice, and they follow me. It is perfectly safe for you to go on in this way even though it looks so wrong, and now I give you another promise: Thine ears shall hear a word behind thee saying, 'This is the way, walk ye in it,' when ye turn to the right hand or to the left."

He paused a moment, and she still leaned against him, speechless with thankfulness and relief at his presence. Then he went on. "Will you bear this too, Much-Afraid? Will you suffer yourself to lose or to be deprived of all that you have gained on this journey to the High Places? Will you go down this path of forgiveness into the Valley of Loss, just because it is the way that I have chosen for you? Will you still trust and still love me?"

She was still clinging to him, and now repeated with all her heart the words of another woman tested long ago. "Entreat me not to leave thee, or to return from following after thee: for whither thou goest I will go; thy people shall be my people and thy God my God." She paused and faltered a moment, then went on in a whisper, "And where thou diest, will I die, and there will I be buried. The Lord do so to me, and more also, if aught but death part thee and me" (Ruth 1:16-17).

So another altar was built at the top of the descent into the Valley of Loss and another stone added to those in the bag she still carried in her bosom. After that they began the downward journey, and as they went she heard her two guides singing softly:

O whither is thy Beloved gone,
Thou fairest among women?
Where doest thou think he has turned aside?
That we may seek him with thee.

The Shepherd himself sang the next verse:

He is gone down into his garden,
To the beds of spices sweet,
For he feedeth among the lilies,
'Tis there we are wont to meet.

Then Much-Afraid herself sang the last two verses, and her heart was so full of joy that even her unmelodious voice seemed changed and sounded as sweet as the others.

So I went down into the garden,
The valley of buds and fruits,
To see if the pomegranates budded,
To look at the vinestock shoots.
And my soul in a burst of rapture,
Or ever I was aware,
Sped swifter than chariot horses,
For lo! He was waiting there.

CANT. 6:1-3

Considering how steep it was, the descent down into the valley seemed surprisingly easy, but perhaps that was because Much-Afraid desired with her whole will to make it in a way that would satisfy and please the Shepherd. The awful glimpse down into the abyss of an existence without him had so staggered and appalled her heart that she felt she could never be quite the same again. However, it had

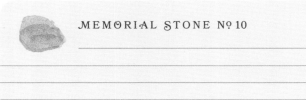

MEMORIAL STONE № 10
_____
_____
_____
_____
_____

WHITHER THOU GOEST, I WILL GO; ...THY PEOPLE SHALL BE MY PEOPLE & THY GOD MY GOD.

RUTH 1:16

opened her eyes to the fact that right down in the depths of her own heart she really had but one passionate desire, not for the things which the Shepherd had promised, but for himself. All she wanted was to be allowed to follow him forever.

Other desires might clamor strongly and fiercely near the surface of her nature, but she knew now that down in the core of her own being she was so shaped that nothing could fit, fill, or satisfy her heart but he himself. "Nothing else really matters," she said to herself, "only to love him and to do what he tells me. I don't know quite why it should be so, but it is. All the time it is suffering to love and sorrow to love, but it is lovely to love him in spite of this, and if I should cease to do so, I should cease to exist." So, as has been said, they reached the valley very quickly.

The next surprising thing was that though the valley did seem at first a little like a prison after the strong bracing air of the mountains, it turned out to be a wonderfully beautiful and peaceful place, very green and with flowers covering the fields and the banks of the river which flowed quietly through it.

Strangely enough, down there in the Valley of Loss, Much-Afraid felt more rested, more peaceful, and more content than anywhere else on the journey. It seemed, too, that her two companions also underwent a strange transformation. They still held her hands, but there was neither suffering nor sorrow in the touch. It was as though they walked close beside her and went hand in hand simply for friendship's sake and for the joy of being together.

Also, they sang continually, sometimes in a language quite different from the one which she had learned from them, but when she asked the meaning of the words they only smiled and shook their heads. This is one of the many songs which all three sang down in the Valley of Loss, and it was another from the collection in the old songbook which Much-Afraid so loved.

I am my Love's and he is mine,
And this is his desire,
That with his beauty I may shine
In radiant attire.
And this will be—when all of me
Is pruned and purged with fire.
Come, my Beloved, let us go
Forth to the waiting field;
And where thy choicest fruit trees grow,
Thy pruning knife now wield
That at thy will and through thy skill
Their richest store may yield.
And spices give a sweet perfume,
And vines show tender shoots,
And all my trees burst forth in bloom,
Fair buds from bitter roots.
There will not I my love deny,
But yield thee pleasant fruits.
CANT. 7:10-13

It is true that when Much-Afraid looked at the mountains on the other side of the valley she wondered how they would ever manage to ascend them, but she found herself content to wait restfully and to wander in the valley as long as the Shepherd chose. One thing in particular comforted her; after the hardness and slipperiness of the way on the mountains, where she had stumbled and limped so painfully, she found that in those quiet green fields she could actually walk without stumbling, and could not feel her wounds and scars and stiffness at all.

All this seemed a little strange because, of course, she really was in the Valley of Loss. Also, apparently, she was farther from the High Places than ever before. She asked the Shepherd about it one day, for the loveliest part of all was that he often walked with them down there, saying with a beautiful smile that it was one of his favorite haunts.

In answer to her question he said, "I am glad that you are learning to appreciate the valley too, but I think it was the altar which you built at the top, Much-Afraid, which has made it so easy for you."

This also rather puzzled her, for she said, "But I have noticed that after the other altars which you told me to build, the way has generally seemed harder and more testing than before."

Again he smiled, but only remarked quietly that the important thing about altars was that they made possibilities of apparent impossibilities, and that it was nice that on this occasion it had brought her peace and not a great struggle. She noticed that he looked at her keenly and rather strangely as he spoke, and though there was a beautiful gentleness in the look, there was also something else which she had seen before, but still did not understand. She thought it held a mixture of two things, not exactly pity—no, that was the wrong word, but a look of wonderful compassion together with unflinching determination.

When she realized that, she thought of some words which one of the Shepherd's servants had spoken down in the Valley of Humiliation before ever the Shepherd had called her to the High Places. He had said, "Love is beautiful, but it is also terrible—terrible in its determination to allow nothing blemished or unworthy to remain in the beloved."

When she remembered this, Much-Afraid thought with a little shiver in her heart, "He will never be content until he makes me what he is determined that I ought to be," and because she was still Much-Afraid and not yet ready to change her name, she added with a pang of fear, "I wonder what he plans to do next, and if it will hurt very much indeed?"

The Place of Anointing

As it happened, the next thing which the Shepherd had planned was very beautiful indeed. Not long after this conversation the path finished its winding way through the valley and led them to the foot of the mountains on the other side to a place where they rose up like a wall, far higher and steeper than the Precipice of Injury.

However, when Much-Afraid and her two companions reached this place they found the Shepherd waiting for them beside a little hut, and lo! just where the cliffs were steepest and highest was an overhead cable suspended between that spot and the summit far above. On this cable hung chairs, in which two could sit side by side and be swung right up to the top without any effort on their part at all. It is true that at first the very sight of these frail-looking aerial chairs swinging along so high above the ground made Much-Afraid feel giddy and panicky. She felt she could never voluntarily place herself in one of them and be swung up that frightful-looking precipice, with only a little footrest and nothing to prevent her casting herself out of the chair if the urge should come upon her.

However, that passed almost at once, for the Shepherd smiled and said, "Come, Much-Afraid, we will seat ourselves in the first two chairs and Sorrow and Suffering will follow in the next. All you have to do is to trust yourself to the chair and be carried in perfect safety up to the place to which I wish to take you and without any struggling and striving on your part."

Much-Afraid stepped into one of the seats, and the Shepherd sat beside her while the two companions occupied the next pair. In a minute they were moving smoothly and steadily toward the High Places which had looked so impossibly out of reach, supported entirely from above, and with nothing to do but rest and enjoy the marvelous view. Though the chairs swung a little in places, they felt no giddiness at all, but went upward and still upward until the valley below looked like a little green carpet and the gleaming white peaks of the Kingdom of Love towered around and above them. Soon they were far above the place to which they had climbed on the mountains opposite, and still they swung along.

When at last they stepped out of the aerial chairs they were in a place more beautiful than anything Much-Afraid had seen before, for though these were not the real High Places of the Kingdom of Love, they had reached the borderland. All around were alps with grassy meadows almost smothered in flowers. Little streams gurgled and splashed between banks of kingcups, while buttercups and cowslips, violets and pink primulae carpeted the ground. Clumps of delicate purple soldanella grew in vivid clusters, and all over the fields, glowing bright as gems, were gentians, more blue than the sky at midday, looking like jewels on a royal robe.

Above were peaks of pure white snow which towered up into a cloudless sky like a roof of sapphire and turquoise. The sun shone so brilliantly it almost seemed that one could see the flowers pushing their way up through the earth and unfolding themselves to receive the glory of its rays. Cowbells and goatbells sounded in every direction, and a multitude of bird notes filled the air, but above the rest was one voice louder and more dominant than them all, and which seemed to fill the whole region.

It was the voice of a mighty waterfall, leaping down

another great cliff which towered above them, and whose rushing waters sprang from the snows in the High Places themselves. It was so unspeakably lovely that neither Much-Afraid nor her companions could utter a word, but stood, drawing deep breaths and filling their lungs with the spicy, pine-scented mountain air.

As they wandered forward, they stooped down at every other step, gently touching the jewel-like flowers or dabbling their fingers in the splashing brooks. Sometimes they just stood still amid the profusion of shining beauty around them and laughed aloud with pure joy. The Shepherd led them across meadows where the warm, scented grass grew nearly waist high, toward the mighty waterfall.

At the foot of the cliffs they found themselves standing in cool shadows with a light spray sometimes splashing their faces, and there the Shepherd bade them stand and look up. There stood Much-Afraid, a tiny figure at the foot of the mighty cliffs, looking up at the great, never-ending rush of waters as they cast themselves down from the High Places. She thought that never before had she seen anything so majestic or so terrifyingly lovely. The height of the rocky lip, over which the waters cast themselves to be dashed in pieces on the rocks below, almost terrified her. At the foot of the fall, the thunderous voice of the waters seemed almost deafening, but it seemed also to be filled with meaning, grand and awesome, beautiful beyond expression.

As she listened, Much-Afraid realized that she was hearing the full majestic harmonies, the whole orchestra as it were, playing the original of the theme song which all the little streamlets had sung far below in the Valley of Humiliation. Now it was uttered by thousands upon thousands of voices, but with grander harmonies than anything heard down in the valleys, yet still the same song.

From the heights we leap and go
To the valleys down below,
Always answering to the call,
To the lowest place of all.

"Much-Afraid," said the Shepherd's voice in her ear, "what do you think of this fall of great waters in their abandonment of self-giving?"

She trembled a little as she answered. "I think they are beautiful and terrible beyond anything which I ever saw before."

"Why terrible?" he asked.

"It is the leap which they have to make, the awful height from which they must cast themselves down to the depths beneath, there to be broken on the rocks. I can hardly bear to watch it."

"Look closer," he said again. "Let your eye follow just one part of the water from the moment when it leaps over the edge until it reaches the bottom."

Much-Afraid did so, and then almost gasped with wonder. Once over the edge, the waters were like winged things, alive with joy, so utterly abandoned to the ecstasy of giving themselves that she could almost have supposed that she was looking at a host of angels floating down on rainbow wings, singing with rapture as they went.

She gazed and gazed, then said, "It looks as though they think it is the loveliest movement in all the world, as though to cast oneself down is to abandon oneself to ecstasy and joy indescribable."

"Yes," answered the Shepherd in a voice vibrant with joy and thanksgiving, "I am glad that you have noticed that, Much-Afraid. These are the Falls of Love, flowing from the High places in the Kingdom above. You will meet with them again. Tell me, does the joy of the waters seem to end when they break on the rock below?"

Again Much-Afraid looked where he pointed and noticed that the lower the water fell, the lighter it seemed to grow, as though it really were lighting down on wings. On reaching the rocks below, all the waters flowed together in a glorious host, forming an exuberant, rushing torrent which swirled triumphantly around and over the rocks.

Laughing and shouting at the top of their voices, they hurried still lower and lower, down through the meadows to the next precipice and the next glorious crisis of their self-giving. From there they would again cast themselves down to the valleys far below. Far from suffering from the rocks, it seemed as though every obstacle in the bed of the torrent was looked upon as another object to be overcome and another lovely opportunity to find a way over or around it. Everywhere was the sound of water, laughing, exulting, shouting in jubilation.

"At first sight perhaps the leap does look terrible," said the Shepherd, "but as you can see, the water itself finds no terror in it, no moment of hesitation or shrinking, only joy unspeakable, and full of glory, because it is the movement natural to it. Self-giving is its life. It has only one desire, to go down and down and give itself with no reserve or holding back of any kind. You can see that as it obeys that glorious urge the obstacles which look so terrifying are perfectly harmless, and indeed only add to the joy and glory of the movement." When he had said this, he led them back to the sunny fields, and gently told them that for the next few days they were to rest themselves there in preparation for the last part of their journey.

On hearing these words, "the last part of the journey," Much-Afraid felt almost as though she would sink to the ground with happiness. Moreover, the Shepherd himself remained there with them the whole time. Not for a single hour was he apart from them, but walked and talked with

them. He taught them many things about the Kingdom to which they were going, and it was as though grace flowed from his lips and sweet ointments and spices were diffused wherever he went. How thankfully Much-Afraid would have stayed there for the rest of her life; she would have cared not more about reaching the High Places, had it not been that she still walked on crooked feet, still had a twisted mouth, still had a fearing heart.

It was not, however, that the sun always shone, even there on that borderland of the High Places. There were days of mist when all the gleaming peaks were completely blotted out by a curtain of cloud, so that if one had never seen them it would have been impossible to be sure that they really existed and were round about, quite close at hand, towering high above the mist and clouds into the clear blue sky above.

Every now and again, however, there would be a rent in the veil of mist, and then, as though framed in an open window, would appear a dazzling whiteness. For a moment one of the vanished peaks would gleam through the opening as if to say, "Be of good courage, we are all here, even though you cannot see us." Then the mist would swirl together again and the window in heaven would close.

On one such occasion the Shepherd said to Much-Afraid, "When you continue your journey there may be much mist and cloud. Perhaps it may even seem as though everything you have seen here of the High Places was just a dream, or the work of your own imagination. But you have seen reality and the mist which seems to swallow it up is the illusion.

"Believe steadfastly in what you have seen. Even if the way up to the High Places appears to be obscured and you are led to doubt whether you are following the right path, remember the promise, 'Thine ears shall hear a word

behind thee, saying, This is the way, walk ye in it, when ye turn to the right hand and when ye turn to the left.' Always go forward along the path of obedience as far as you know it until I intervene, even if it seems to be leading you where you fear I could never mean you to go.

"Remember, Much-Afraid, what you have seen before the mist blotted it out. Never doubt that the High Places are there, towering up above you, and be quite sure that whatever happens I mean to bring you up there exactly as I have promised." As he finished speaking another rent appeared in the curtain of mist, and one of the peaks of the High Places framed in blue sky shone down on them.

Before the curtain closed again Much-Afraid stooped down and picked a few of the gentians growing near her feet as a reminder of what she had seen, for, said she to herself, "These actually grew on the lower slopes of the High Places and are an earnest that though the peaks may again become invisible they are there all the time."

On the last day they stayed there the Shepherd did a very wonderful thing. He took Much-Afraid apart by herself and carried her right up to the summit of one of the High Places—in the Kingdom of Love itself. He took her to a high peak, dazzling white, uplifted like a great throne with numberless other peaks grouped round about.

Up there on the mountaintop he was transfigured before her, and she knew him then to be what she had dimly sensed all along—the King of Love himself, King of the whole Realm of Love. He was clothed in a white garment glistening in its purity, but over it he wore a robe of purple and blue and scarlet studded with gold and precious gems. On his head he wore the crown royal, but as Much-Afraid bowed herself and knelt at his feet to worship, the face that looked down upon her was that of the Shepherd whom she had loved and followed from the very low places up to the heights. His eyes were still full of gentleness and tenderness but also of strength and power and authority.

Putting out his hand, without a word he lifted her up and led her to a place where on the topmost pinnacle of all they could look right out on the whole realm around them. Standing there beside him and so happy as to be scarcely conscious of herself at all, Much-Afraid looked out over the Kingdom of Love. Far, far below were the valleys and the plains and the great sea and the desert. She even thought she could recognize the Valley of Humiliation itself, where she had lived so long and had first learned to know the Shepherd, but that seemed so long ago it was like remembering another existence altogether.

All around her, in every direction, were the snowy peaks of the High Places. She could see that the bases of all these mountains were extremely precipitous and that higher up they were all clothed with forests, then the green slopes of the higher alps and then the snow. Wherever she looked, the slopes at that season of the year were covered with pure white flowers through whose half-transparent petals the sun shone, turning them to burning whiteness.

In the heart of each flower was a crown of pure gold. These white-robed hosts scented the slopes of the High Places with a perfume sweeter than any she had ever breathed before. All had their faces and golden crowns turned down the mountains as if looking at the valleys, multitudes upon multitudes of them, which no man could number, like "a great cloud of witnesses," all stooping forward to watch what was going on in the world below. Wherever the King and his companion walked, these white-robed flowers bowed beneath their feet and rose again, buoyant and unsullied, but exuding a perfume richer and sweeter than before.

On the utmost pinnacle to which he led her was an altar of pure gold, flashing in the sun with such splendor that she could not look at it but had to turn her eyes away at once, though she did perceive that a fire burned on it and a cloud of smoke perfumed with incense rose from it.

Then the King told her to kneel and with a pair of golden tongs brought a piece of burning coal from off the altar. Touching her with it he said, "Lo! this hath touched thy lips; and thine iniquity is taken away, and thy sin purged" (Isa. 6:7).

It seemed to her that a burning flame of fire too beautiful and too terrible to bear went through her whole being, and Much-Afraid lost consciousness and remembered no more.

When she recovered she found that the Shepherd was carrying her in his arms and they were back on the lower slopes of the borderland. The royal robes and the crown were gone, but something of the expression on his face remained, the look of utmost authority and power. Above them towered the peaks, while everything below was shrouded in cloud and mist.

When he found that she was sufficiently recovered, the Shepherd took her by the hand, and they walked together down into the white mist and through a little wood where the trees were scarcely visible and there was no sound but drops of water splashing onto the ground. When in the middle of the wood a bird burst into song. They could not see it for the mist, but high and clear and indescribably sweet the bird sang and called the same series of little notes over and over again. They seemed to form a phrase constantly repeated, always with a higher chirrup at the end which sounded just like a little chuckling laugh. It seemed to Much-Afraid that this was the song the bird was singing:

He's gotten the victory, Hurrah!
He's gotten the victory, Hurrah!

The wood rang with the jubilant notes, and they both stood still among the dripping trees to listen.

"Much-Afraid," the Shepherd said, "you have had a glimpse of the Kingdom into which I am going to bring you. Tomorrow you and your companions start on the last part of your journey which will bring you thither."

Then with wonderful tenderness he spoke words which seemed too glorious to be true. "Thou hast a little strength and hast kept my word, and hast not denied my name. . . . Behold I will make thine enemies to come and worship before thy feet, and to know that I have loved thee. Behold, I come quickly: Hold fast that which thou hast, that no man take thy crown, and she that overcometh will I make a pillar in the temple of my God, and she shall go no more out: and I will write upon her the name of my God . . . I will write upon her my new name" (Rev. 3:8-12).

It was then that Much-Afraid took courage to ask him something which she had never dared ask before. With her hand held in his she said, "My Lord, may I ask one thing? Is the time at last soon coming when you will fulfill the promise that you gave me?"

He said very gently, yet with great joy, "Yes—the time is not long now. Dare to begin to be happy. If you will go forward in the way before you, you will soon receive the promise, and I will give you your heart's desire. It is not long now, Much-Afraid."

So they stood in the mist-filled wood, she trembling with hope and unable to say a word, worshiping and wondering if she had seen a vision, or if this thing had really happened. Upon his face was a look which she would not have understood even if she had seen it, but she was too dazed with happiness even to look at him. High over the dripping trees the little bird still sang his jubilant song, "He's gotten the victory," and then in a burst of trills and chuckles, "Hurrah! Hurrah! Hurrah!"

A little later they were down in the meadows where Sorrow and her sister were waiting for their return. It was time to go forward on the journey, but after the Shepherd had blessed them and was turning to go his way again, Suffering and Sorrow suddenly knelt before him and asked softly, "Lord, what place is this where we have been resting and refreshing ourselves during these past days?"

He answered very quietly, "This is the place to which I bring my beloved, that they may be anointed in readiness for their burial."

Much-Afraid did not hear these words, for she was walking a little ahead, repeating over and over again, "He said, 'Dare to begin to be happy, for the time is not long now, and I will give you your heart's desire.'"

I WILL WRITE UPON HIM THE NAME OF MY GOD...I WILL WRITE UPON HIM MY NEW NAME.

REVELATION 3:12

The Floods

THE PATH THEY FOLLOWED did not go straight up to the heights but sloped gently up the mountainside. The mist still shrouded everything, and indeed grew a little thicker. All three walked in silence, occupied with different thoughts. Much-Afraid was thinking of the promise the Shepherd so recently had given her, "Behold, I come quickly . . . and will give thee thy heart's desire." Suffering and Sorrow perhaps were thinking of the answer they had received to the question asked of him at parting. Whether or not this was so there was no indication, for they walked in complete silence, though the help they gave their lame companion was, had she noticed it, even more gentle and untiring than before.

Toward evening they came to another log cabin standing at the side of the path with the Shepherd's secret mark inscribed upon the door, so they knew that they were to rest there for the night.

Once inside they noticed that someone must have been there quite recently, for a fire was burning brightly on the hearth and a kettle of water was singing on the hob. The table, too, was laid for three, and a supply of bread and fruit upon it. Evidently their arrival had been expected and these kindly preparations made, but of the one who had thus gone in the way before them there was no sign. They washed themselves and then sat down at the table, gave thanks, and ate of the prepared meal. Then, being weary, they lay down to rest and immediately fell asleep.

How long she had slept Much-Afraid could not tell, but she woke suddenly while it was still quite dark. Her companions slumbered peacefully beside her, but she knew that someone had called her. She waited in silence, then a Voice said: "Much-Afraid."

"Behold me, here I am, my Lord," she answered.

"Much-Afraid," said the Voice, "take now the promise you received when I called you to follow me to the High Places, and take the natural longing for human love which you found already growing in your heart when I planted my own love there and go up into the mountains to the place that I shall show you. Offer them there as a Burnt Offering unto me."

There was a long silence before Much-Afraid's trembling voice spoke through the darkness.

"My Lord—am I understanding you right?"

"Yes," answered the Voice. "Come now to the entrance of the hut and I will show you where you are to go."

Without waking the two beside her, she rose silently, opened the door of the hut, and stepped outside.

Everything was still shrouded in mist, and the mountains were completely invisible, swallowed up in darkness and cloud. As she looked, the mist parted in one place and a little window appeared through which the moon and one star shone brightly. Just below them was a white peak, glimmering palely. At its foot was the rocky ledge over which the great waterfall leaped and rushed down to the slopes below. Only the lip of rock over which it poured itself was visible, all below being shrouded in the mist.

Then came the Voice, "That is the appointed place."

Much-Afraid looked, and replied, "Yes, Lord. Behold me—I am thy handmaiden, I will do according to thy word."

She did not lie down again, but stood at the door of the hut waiting for daybreak. It seemed to her that the voice of the fall now filled the whole night and was thundering through her trembling heart, reverberating and shouting through every part and repeating again and again, "Take now the promise that I gave you, and the natural human love in your heart, and offer them for a burnt offering."

With the first glimmer of dawn she bent over her sleeping companions and said, "We must start at once. I have received commandment to go up to the place where the great fall pours itself over the precipice."

They rose immediately, and after hurriedly eating a meal to strengthen themselves, they started on their way. The path led straight up the mountainside toward the thunderous voice of the fall, though everything was still shrouded in mist and cloud and the fall itself remained invisible.

As the hours passed they continued to climb, though the path was now steeper than ever before. In the distance thunder began to roll and flashes of lightning rent the veil of mist. Suddenly, higher up on the path, they heard the sound of running feet, slipping and scraping on the rocks and stones. They stopped and pressed themselves closely to one side of the narrow path to allow the runners to pass, then out of the ghostly mist appeared first Fear, then Bitterness, followed by Resentment, Pride, and Self-Pity.

They were running as though for their lives, and as they reached the three women they shouted, "Back! Turn back at once! The avalanches are falling ahead, and the whole mountainside is shaking as though it will fall too. Run for your lives!"

Without waiting for an answer, they clattered roughly past and fled down the mountainside.

"What are we to do?" asked Suffering and Sorrow, apparently at a loss for the very first time. "Shall we turn back to the hut and wait until the avalanches and the storm are over?"

"No," said Much-Afraid in a low, steady voice, speaking for the first time since she had called them to rise and follow her. "No, we must not turn back. I have received a commandment to go up to the place where the great fall pours over the rock."

Then the Voice spoke close at hand. "There is a place prepared for you here beside the path. Wait there until the storm is over."

In the rocky wall beside them was a little cave so low that it could be entered only if they stooped right down, and with just enough room for them to crouch inside. Side by side, they sat huddled together, then all of a sudden the storm burst over them in frightful fury. The mountains reverberated with thunder and with the sound of falling rocks and great avalanches. The lightning flashed incessantly and ran along the ground in sizzling flames.

Then the rains descended and the floods came, and the winds blew and beat upon the mountains until everything around them seemed to be shivering and quaking and falling. Flood waters rushed down the steep cliffs and

a torrent poured over the rocks which projected over the cave so that the whole entrance was closed with a waterfall, but not a single drop fell inside the cave where the three sat together on the ground.

After they had been there for some time and the storm, far from abating, seemed to be increasing in strength, Much-Afraid silently put her hand in her bosom and drew out the leather bag which she always carried. Emptying the little heap of stones and pebbles into her lap, she looked at them. They were the memorial stones from all the altars which she had built along the way, from the time that she stood beside the Shepherd at the pool and allowed him to plant the thorn in her heart and all along the journey until that moment of crouching in a narrow cave upon which the whole mountain seemed to be ready to topple. Nothing was left to her but a command to offer up the promise on which she had staked her all, on the strength of which she had started on the journey.

She looked at the little pile in her lap and asked herself dully, "Shall I throw them away? Were they not all worthless promises which he gave me on the way here?" Then with icy fingers she picked up the first stone and repeated the first words that he had spoken to her beside the pool. "I will make thy feet like hinds' feet and set thee upon thine High Places" (Hab. 3:19). She held the stone in her hand for a long time, then said slowly, "I have not received hinds' feet, but I am on higher places than ever I imagined possible, and if I die up here, what does it matter? I will not throw it away."

She put the stone back in the bag, picked up the next and repeated, "What I do thou knowest not now; but thou shalt know hereafter" (John 13:7); and she gave a little sob and said, "Half at least of that is true, and who knows whether the other half is true or not—but I will not throw it away."

Picking up the third stone, she quoted, "This is not unto death, but for the glory of God" (John 11:4). "Not unto death," she repeated, "even though he says, 'Offer the promise as a Burnt Offering'?" But she dropped the stone back into the bag and took the fourth. "Bread corn is bruised . . . but no one crushes it forever" (Isa. 28:28). "I cannot part with that," she said, replaced it in the bag, and took the fifth. "Cannot I do with you as the Potter?

saith the Lord" (Jer. 18:6). "Yes," said she, and put it back into the bag.

Taking the sixth, she repeated, "O thou afflicted, tossed with tempest, and not comforted, behold, I will lay thy stones with fair colors . . ." (Isa. 54:11), then could go no farther but wept bitterly. "How could I part with that?" she asked herself, and she put it in the bag with the others, and took the seventh. "My sheep hear my voice, and they follow me" (John 10:27). "Shall I not throw this one away?" she asked herself. "Have I really heard his voice, or have I been deceiving myself all the time?"

Then as she thought of his face when he gave her that promise she replaced it in the bag saying, "I will keep it. How can I let it go?" and took the eighth. "Now shalt thou see what I will do" (Ex. 6:1). Remembering the precipice which had seemed so terribly impossible and how he had brought her to the top, she put the stone with the others and took the ninth. "God is not a man, that he should lie . . . hath he said and shall he not do it? or hath he spoken, and shall he not make it good?" (Num. 23:19).

For a very long time she sat trembling with that stone in her hand, but in the end she said, "I have already given the only answer possible when I told him, 'If thou canst, thou mayest deceive me.'"

Then she dropped the icy-cold little pebble into the bag and took the tenth. "Thine ears shall hear a word behind thee, saying, 'This is the way, walk ye in it, when ye turn to the right hand, and when ye turn to the left'" (Isa. 30:21). At that she shuddered, but after a while added, "Thou hast a little strength, and hast not denied my name . . . Hold that fast which thou hast, that no man take thy crown" (Rev. 3:8, 11).

Returning the tenth stone to the bag, after a long pause she picked up an ugly little stone lying on the floor of the cave and dropped it in beside the other ten, saying, "Though he slay me, yet will I trust in him" (Job 13:15). Tying up the bag again, she said, "Though everything in the world should tell me that they are worthless—yet I cannot part with them," and put the bag once again in her bosom.

Sorrow and her sister had been sitting silently beside her watching intently as she went over the little heap of stones in her lap. Both gave a strange laugh, as though of relief and thankfulness, and said together, "The rain descended, and the floods came, and the winds blew, and beat upon the house; and it fell not: for it was founded upon a rock" (Matt. 7:25).

By this time, the rain had ceased, the cataract was no longer pouring over the rocks, and only a light mist remained. The rolling of the thunder and the roar of the avalanches were fading away into the distance, and as they

 MEMORIAL STONE № 11

looked out of the cave, up from the depths beneath came through the wreaths of mist the clear, jubilant notes of a bird. It might have been brother to that which sang in the dripping woods at the foot of the High Places:

 He's gotten the victory, Hurrah!
He's gotten the victory. Hurrah!

As the pure clear notes came floating up to them the icy coldness in the heart of Much-Afraid broke, then melted away. She pressed her hands convulsively against the little bag of stones as though it contained priceless treasure which she had thought lost, and said to her companions. "The storm is over. Now we can go on our way."

From that place on, it was very steep going, for the path now went straight up the mountainside, so straight and steep that often Much-Afraid could hardly do more than crawl forward on hands and knees. All along she had hoped that the higher she went and the nearer she got to the High Places, the stronger she would become and the less she would stumble, but it was quite otherwise.

The higher they went, the more conscious she was that her strength was leaving her, and the weaker she grew, the more she stumbled. She could not help dimly realizing that this was not the case with her companions. The higher they went, the more vigorous and strong they seemed to become, and this was good, because often they had almost to carry Much-Afraid, for she seemed utterly spent and exhausted. Because of this they made very slow progress indeed.

On the second day they came to a place where a little hollow in the mountainside formed a tiny plateau. Here a spring bubbled out of the cliff and trickled across the hollow and down the side of the mountain in a little waterfall. As they paused to rest, the Voice said to Much-Afraid, "Drink of the brook at the side of the way and be strengthened."

Stooping down at the spring where it bubbled up from between the rocks, she filled her mouth with the water, but as soon as she swallowed it she found it so burning and bitter that her stomach rejected it altogether and she was unable to retain it. She knelt by the spring, gasping for a moment, and then said very quietly and softly through the silence, "My Lord, it is not that I will not, but that I cannot drink of this cup."

"There is a tree growing beside this spring of Marah,"

MEMORIAL STONE № 12

_____

_____

_____

_____

answered the Voice. "Break off a piece of branch, and when you have cast it into the waters they will be sweetened."

Much-Afraid looked on the other side of the spring and saw a little stunted thorn tree with but one branch growing on either side of the splintered trunk, like the arms of a cross. They were covered all over with long sharp spines.

Suffering stepped forward, broke off a piece of the thorn tree, and brought it to Much-Afraid, who took it from her hand and cast it into the water. On doing this she stooped her head again to drink. This time she found that the stinging, burning bitterness was gone, and though the water was not sweet, she could drink it easily. She drank thirstily and found that it must have contained curative properties, for almost at once she was wonderfully refreshed and strengthened. Then she picked up her twelfth and last stone there beside the water of Marah and put it into her bag.

After they had rested a little while she was able to resume the journey, and for a time was so much stronger that although the way was even steeper than before, she was not nearly so faint and exhausted. This greatly comforted her, for by that time she had only one desire in her heart, to reach the place appointed and fulfill the command which had been given her before her strength ebbed away altogether. On the third day, "they lifted up their eyes and saw the place afar off," the great rock cliff and the waterfall, and continuing up the rocky path, at midday they came through the shrouding mist to the place which had been appointed.

Grave on the Mountains

THE PATH LED FORWARD to the edge of a yawning chasm, then stopped dead. This grave-like gorge yawned before them in each direction as far as they could see completely cutting off all further progress. It was so filled with cloud and mist that they could not see how deep it was, nor could they see across to the other side, but spread before them like a great gaping grave, waiting to swallow them up. For a moment Much-Afraid wondered whether this could be the place, after all, but as they halted on the edge of the canyon, they could plainly hear the sound of mighty, swirling waters, and she realized that they must be standing somewhere near the lip of the great fall and that this was indeed the place appointed.

Looking at her companions, she asked quietly, "What must we do now? Can we jump across to the other side?"

"No," they said, "it would be impossible."

"What, then, are we to do?" she asked.

"We must leap down into the canyon," was the answer.

"Of course," said Much-Afraid at once. "I did not realize at first, but that is the thing to do."

Then for the last time on that journey (though she did not know it at the time) she held out her hand to her two companions that they might help her. But this time she was so weak and exhausted that instead of taking her hands, they came close up to her and put their hands beneath her arms so that she leaned with her full weight against them. Thus with Suffering and Sorrow supporting her, Much-Afraid cast herself down into the yawning grave.

The place into which they had thrown themselves was deep, and had she been alone she must have been badly hurt by the fall. However, her companions were so strong that the jump did not seem to harm them at all, and they bore her so easily between them and broke the fall so gently that she was no more than bruised and shaken. Then, because the canyon was so filled with mist and cloud that nothing was visible, they began to feel their way slowly forward and saw, looming up before them, a flat, oblong rock. On reaching it, they found it to be some kind of stone altar with the indistinct figure of someone standing behind it.

"This is the place," said Much-Afraid quietly. "This is where I am to make my offering." She went up to the altar and knelt down. "My Lord," she said softly through the mist. "Will you come to me now and help me to make my burnt offering as you have commanded me?"

But for the first time on all that journey there seemed to be no answer—no answer at all—and the Shepherd did not come.

She knelt there quite alone in the cold, clammy mist, beside the desolate altar in this valley of shadow, and into her mind came the words which Bitterness had flung at her long before when she walked the shores of loneliness: "Sooner or later, when he gets you up on the wild places of the mountains he will put you on some sort of a cross and abandon you to it."

It seemed that in a way Bitterness had been right, thought Much-Afraid to herself, only he had been too ignorant to know and she too foolish at that time to understand that in all the world only one thing really mattered, to do the will of the one she followed and loved, no matter what it involved or cost. Strangely enough, as she knelt there by the altar, seemingly abandoned at that last tremendous crisis, there was no sign or sound of the presence of her enemies.

The grave up on the mountains is at the very edge of the High Places and beyond the reach of Pride and Bitterness and Resentment and Self-Pity, yes, and of Fear too, as though she were in another world altogether, for they can never cast themselves down into that grave. She knelt there feeling neither despair nor hope. She knew now without a shadow of doubt that there would be no Angel to call from heaven to say that the sacrifice need not be made, and this knowledge caused her neither dread nor shrinking.

She felt nothing but a great stillness in which only one desire remained, to do that which he had told her, simply because he had asked it of her. The cold, dull desolation which had filled her heart in the cave was gone completely; one flame burned there steadily, the flame of concentrated desire to do his will. Everything else had died down and fallen into ashes.

After she had waited for little and still he had not come, she put out her hand and with one final effort of failing strength grasped the natural human love and desire growing in her heart and struggled to tear them out. At the first touch it was as though anguish pierced through her every nerve and fiber, and she knew with a pang almost of despair that the roots had wound and twined and thrust themselves into every part of her being. Though she put forth all her remaining strength in the most desperate effort to wrench them out, not a single rootlet stirred.

For the first time she felt something akin to fear and panic. She was not able to do this thing which he had asked of her. Having reached the altar at last, she was powerless to obey. Turning to those who had been her guides and helpers all the way up the mountains, she asked for their help, and for them to do what she could not for herself, to tear the plant out of her heart. For the first time Suffering and Sorrow shook their heads.

"We have done all that we can for you," they answered, "but this we cannot do."

At that the indistinct figure behind the altar stepped forward and said quietly, "I am the priest of this altar—I will take it out of your heart if you wish."

Much-Afraid turned toward him instantly. "Oh, thank you," she said. "I beg you to do so."

He came and stood beside her, his form indistinct and blurred by the mist, and then she continued entreatingly, "I am a very great coward. I am afraid that the pain may cause me to try to resist you. Will you bind me to the altar in some way so that I cannot move? I would not like to be found struggling while the will of my Lord is done."

There was complete silence in the cloud-filled canyon for a moment or two, then the priest answered, "It is well said. I will bind you to the altar." Then he bound her hand and foot.

When he had finished, Much-Afraid lifted her face toward the High Places which were quite invisible and spoke quietly through the mist. "My Lord, behold me— here I am, in the place thou didst send me to—doing the thing thou didst tell me to do, for where thou diest, will I die, and there will I be buried; the Lord do so to me, and more also, if aught but death part thee and me." (Ruth 1:17).

Still there was silence, a silence as of the grave, for indeed she was in the grave of her own hopes and still without the promised hinds' feet, still outside the High Places with even the promise to be laid down on the altar. This was the place to which the long, heartbreaking journey had led her. Yet just once more before she laid it down on the altar, Much-Afraid repeated the glorious promise which had been the cause of her starting for the High Places. "The Lord God is my strength, and he will make my feet like hinds' feet and he will make me to walk up on mine High Places. To the chief singer on my stringed instruments" (Hab. 3:19).

The priest put forth a hand of steel, right into her heart. There was a sound of rending and tearing, and the human love, with all its myriad rootlets and fibers, came forth.

He held it for a moment and then said, "Yes, it was ripe for removal, the time had come. There is not a rootlet torn or missing."

When he had said this he cast it down on the altar and spread his hands above it. There came a flash of fire which seemed to rend the altar; after that, nothing but ashes remained, either of the love itself, which had been so deeply planted in her heart, or of the suffering and sorrow which had been her companions on that long, strange journey. A sense of utter, overwhelming rest and peace engulfed Much-Afraid. At last, the offering had been made and there was nothing left to be done. When the priest had unbound her she leaned forward over the ashes on the altar and said with complete thanksgiving, "It is finished."

Then, utterly exhausted, she fell asleep.

What troubles weigh heavily on your soul? Take comfort in
knowing the joy of the morning is coming soon. Does the darkness
seem more hopeful with the Good Shepherd by your side?

_____

_____

_____

_____

PART TWO

"Joy cometh in the morning."

PSALM 30:5

Healing Streams

WHEN AT LAST MUCH-AFRAID AWOKE, the sun was high in the sky, and she looked out through the mouth of the cave in which she found herself lying. Everything was shimmering in a blaze of radiant sunshine which burnished every object with glory. She lay still a little longer, collecting her thoughts and trying to understand where she was.

The rocky cave into which the sunbeams were pouring was warm and quiet and drenched with the sweet perfume of spikenard, frankincense, and myrrh. This perfume she gradually realized was emanating from the wrappings which covered her. She gently pushed back the folds, sat up, and looked about her. Then the memory of all that had happened returned to her.

She and her two companions had come to a cloud-filled canyon high up on the mountains and to an altar

of sacrifice, and the priest had wrenched out of her heart her flower of human love and burned it on the altar. On remembering that, she glanced down at her breast and saw it was covered with a cloth soaked in the spices whose perfume stole out and filled the cave with sweetness. She pushed the cloth aside a little curiously and was astonished to find no trace of a wound—not even a scar, nor was there any hint of pain or aching or stiffness anywhere in her body.

Rising quietly, she went outside, then stood still and looked about her. The canyon, which had been so shrouded in mist that nothing had been distinguishable, now shimmered in the golden sunlight. Soft, verdant grass grew everywhere, starred with gentians and other little jewel-like flowers of every variety. There were banks of sweet-smelling thyme, moss, and myrtle along the sides of the rocky walls, and everything sparkled with dew.

In the center of the canyon, at a little distance from the cave, was the long stone altar to which she had been bound, but in the sunlight she saw that the flowers and mosses grew all about it and clothed its sides with verdure. Little birds hopped about here and there, scattering the dewdrops off the grasses and chirping merrily as they preened their plumage.

One was perched on the altar itself, its little throat throbbing as it trilled forth a song of joy, but the most

beautiful and wonderful thing of all was that out from under the rock altar there gushed a great "river of water, clear as crystal." It then flowed in a series of cascades and through rock pools right through the canyon till it came to a broad lip of rock, over which it poured with a noise of shouting and tumultuous gladness. She was at the very source of the great fall and knew now that it flowed from under the altar to which the priest had bound her.

For some time she stood looking about her, her heart leaping and thrilling with a growing joy which was beyond her understanding and a peace indescribably sweet which seemed to enfold her. She was quite alone in the canyon. There were no signs of her companions Sorrow and Suffering nor of the priest of the altar. The only things which breathed and moved in the canyon beside herself were the cheerful little chirping birds and the insects and butterflies flittering among the flowers. High overhead was a cloudless sky, against which the peaks of the High Places shone dazzlingly white.

The first thing she did, after she had taken in her surroundings, was to step toward the river which gushed out from under the altar. It drew her irresistibly. She stooped down when she got to the bank and dabbled her fingers in the crystal water. It was icy cold, but it sent a shock of ecstasy tingling through her body, and without further delay she put off the white linen robe she was wearing and stepped into one of the rocky pools. Never had she experienced anything so delicious and exhilarating. It was like immersing herself in a stream of bubbling life. When at last she again stepped out of the pool she was immediately dry and tingling from head to foot with a sense of perfect well-being.

As she stood on the mossy bank by the pool she happened to glance down and noticed for the first time that her feet were no longer the crooked, ugly things which they always had been, but were "straight feet," perfectly formed, shining white against the soft green grass.

Then she remembered the healing stream of which the Shepherd had spoken, which gushed out of the ground on the High Places. Stepping straight back into the pool with a shock of sweetest pleasure and putting her head beneath the clear waters, she splashed them about her face. Then she found a little pool among the rocks, still and clear as a mirror. Kneeling down, she looked into its unruffled surface and saw her face quite clearly. It was true, the ugly, twisted mouth had vanished and the face she saw reflected back by the water was as relaxed and perfect as the face of a little child.

After that she began to wander about the canyon and noticed wild strawberries and blueberries and other small berries growing on the banks. She found a handful of these as refreshing and sustaining a meal as ever she had eaten.

Then she came to the lip of the rock cliff over which the river cast itself, and stood a long time watching the water as it leaped over the edge with the noise of its tumultuous joy drowning every other sound. She saw how the sun glorified the crystal waters as they went swirling downward and far below she saw the green alps where the Shepherd had led her and where they had stood at the foot of this same fall. She felt completely encompassed by peace, and a great inner quietness and contentment drowned every feeling of curiosity, loneliness and anticipation.

She did not think about the future at all. It was enough to be there in that quiet canyon, hidden away high up in the mountains with the river of life flowing beside her, and to rest and recover herself after the long journey. After a little she lay down on a mossy bank and slept, and when she woke again, bathed herself in the river. So the long, quiet day passed like a sweet dream while she rested and bathed and refreshed herself at intervals with the berries and then slept again.

When at last the shadows lengthened and the sun sank in the west and the snow peaks glowed glorious in rose and flame color she went back into the cave, laid herself down among the spice-perfumed coverings and slept as deeply and dreamlessly as she had the first night when the priest laid her there to rest.

Hinds' Feet

Oɴ ᴛʜᴇ ᴛʜɪʀᴅ ᴅᴀʏ, while it was still almost dark, she woke suddenly, and sprang to her feet with a shock of joy tingling through her. She had not heard her name called, had not even been conscious of a voice, yet she knew that she had been called. Some mysterious, poignantly sweet summons had reached her, a summons which she knew instinctively she had been awaiting ever since she woke up for the first time in the cave. She stepped outside into the fragrant summer night. The morning star hung low in the sky, and in the east the first glimmer of dawn appeared. From somewhere close at hand a solitary bird uttered one clear, sweet note and a light breeze stirred over the grasses. Otherwise there was no sound save the voice of the great waterfall.

Then it came again—tingling through her—a call ringing down from some high place above. Standing there in the pale dawn, she looked eagerly around. Every nerve in her body surged with desire to respond to the call, and she felt her feet and legs tingling with an almost irresistible urge to go bounding up the mountains, but where was the way out of the canyon? The walls seemed to rise smooth and almost perpendicular on all sides, except at the end which was blocked by the waterfall.

Then, as she stood straining every nerve to find a possible means of exit, up from a nearby mossy bank sprang a mountain hart with the hind close behind him, just as she had seen them at the foot of the great Precipice of Injury. As she watched, the hart sprang onto the altar of rock, and from there with a great leap he reached a projecting ledge on the wall on the farther side of the ravine. Then, closely followed by the hind, he began springing up the great wall of the canyon.

Much-Afraid did not hesitate one instant. In a moment she was on the rock altar herself, the next, with a flying leap, she, too, reached the ledge on the wall. Then, using the same footholds as the hart and the hind, leaping and springing in a perfect ecstasy of delight, she followed them up the cliff, the hooves of the deer ringing on the rocks before her like little silver hammers.

In a moment or two all three were at the top of the canyon, and she was leaping up the mountainside toward the peak above, from which the summons had come. The rosy light in the east brightened, the snow on the summits of the mountains caught the glow and flushed like fire, and as she skipped and jumped from rock to rock excitedly the first sunbeams streamed over the mountaintop. He was there—standing on the peak—just as she had known he would be, strong and grand and glorious in the beauty of the sunrise, holding out both hands and calling to her with a great laugh, "You—with the hinds' feet—jump over here."

She gave one last flying spring, caught his hands and landed beside him on the topmost peak of the mountain. Around them in every direction towered other and greater ranges of snow mountains, whose summits soared into the sky higher than her sight could follow them. He was crowned, and dressed in royal robes, just as she had seen him once before when he had carried her up to the High Places, and had touched her with the live coal from off the golden Altar of Love. Then his face had been stern in its majesty and gravity, now it was alight with glory of joy which excelled anything which she had ever imagined.

"At last," he said, as she knelt speechless at his feet, "at last you are here and the 'night of weeping is over and joy comes to you in the morning.'" Then, lifting her up, he continued, "This is the time when you are to receive the fulfillment of the promises. Never am I to call you Much-Afraid again." At that he laughed again and said, "I will write upon her a new name, the name of her God. The Lord God is a sun and shield: the Lord will give grace and glory: no good thing will he withhold from them that walk uprightly" (Psa. 84:11). "This is your new name," he declared. "From henceforth you are Grace and Glory."

Still she could not speak, but stood silent with joy and thanksgiving and awe and wonder.

Then he went on, "Now for the flower of Love and for the promise that when it blooms you will be loved in return."

Grace and Glory spoke for the first time. "My Lord and King," she said softly, "there is no flower of Love to bloom in my heart. It was burned to ashes on the altar at thy command."

"No flower of Love?" he repeated, and laughed again so gently and joyfully that she could hardly bear it. "That is strange, Grace and Glory. How, then, did you get here? You are right on the High Places, in the Kingdom of Love itself. Open your heart and let us see what is there."

At his word she laid bare her heart, and out came the sweetest perfume she had ever breathed and filled all the air around them with its fragrance. There in her heart was a plant whose shape and form could not be seen because it was covered all over with pure white, almost transparent blooms, from which the fragrance poured forth.

Grace and Glory gave a little gasp of wonder and thankfulness. "How did it get there, my Lord and King?" she exclaimed.

"Why, I planted it there myself," was his laughing answer. "Surely you remember, down there by the sheep pool in the Valley of Humiliation, on the day that you promised to go with me to the High Places. It is the flower from the thorn-shaped seed."

"Then, my Lord, what was the plant which the priest tore out of my heart when I was bound to the altar?"

"Do you remember, Grace and Glory, when you looked into your heart beside the pool, and found that my kind of love was not there at all—only the plant of Longing-to-be-loved?"

She nodded wonderingly.

"That was the natural human love which I tore out from your heart when the time was ripe and it was loose enough to be uprooted altogether so that the real Love could grow there alone and fill your whole heart."

"You tore it out!" she repeated slowly and wonderingly, and then, "O my Lord and King, were you the priest? Were you there all the time, when I thought you had forsaken me?"

He bowed his head and she took his hands in hers, the scarred hands which had sown the thorn-shaped seed in her heart, and the hands with the grasp of steel which had torn out that love which had been the cause of all her pain, and kissed them while tears of joy fell on them.

"And now for the promise," said he, "that when Love flowers in your heart you shall be loved again." Taking her hand in his, he said, "Behold I have set my love upon thee and thou art mine . . . yea, I have loved thee with an everlasting love: therefore with loving-kindness have I drawn thee" (Jer. 31:3). After that he said, "Give me the

bag of stones of remembrance that you have gathered on your journey, Grace and Glory."

She took it out and passed it to him and then he bade her hold out her hands. On doing so, he opened the little purse and emptied the contents into her hands. Then she gasped again with bewilderment and delight, for instead of the common, ugly stones she had gathered from the altars along the way, there fell into her hands a heap of glorious, sparkling jewels, very precious and very beautiful. As she stood there, half-dazzled by the glory of the flashing gems, she saw in his hand a circlet of pure gold.

"O thou who wast afflicted, tossed with tempest and not comforted," he said, "behold I lay thy stones with fair colors."

First he picked out of her hand one of the biggest and most beautiful of the stones—a sapphire, shining like the pavement of heaven, and set it in the center of the golden circlet. Then, taking a fiery, blood-red ruby, he set it on one side of the sapphire and an emerald on the other. After that he took the other stones—twelve in all—and arranged them on the circlet, then set it upon her head.

At that moment Grace and Glory remembered the cave in which she had sheltered from the floods, and how nearly she had succumbed to the temptation to discard as worthless those stones which now shone with glory and splendor in the crown upon her head. She remembered, too, the words which had sounded in her ears and had restrained her, "Hold fast that thou hast, that no man take thy crown." Supposing she had thrown them away, had

I HAVE LOVED THEE WITH AN EVERLASTING LOVE: THEREFORE WITH LOVINGKINDNESS HAVE I DRAWN THEE.

JEREMIAH 31:3

discarded her trust in his promises, had gone back on her surrenders to his will? There could have been no jewels now to his praise and glory, and no crown for her to wear.

She marveled at the grace and love and tenderness and patience which had led and trained and guarded and kept poor faltering Much-Afraid, which had not allowed her to turn back, and which now changed all her trials into glory. Then she heard him speaking again and this time the smile on his face was almost more joyful than before.

"Hearken, O daughter, and consider, and incline thine ear; forget also thine own people, and thy father's house; so shall the King greatly desire thy beauty: for he is thy Lord; and worship thou him. . . . The King's daughter is all glorious within. She shall be brought unto the King in clothing of wrought gold, in raiment of needlework. The virgins, her companions that follow her, shall be brought unto thee. With gladness and rejoicing shall they be brought: they shall enter into the King's palace" (Psa. 45:10-15). Then he added, "Now that you are to live with me here on the High Places, to go where I go, and to share my work in the valley below, it is fitting, Grace and Glory, that you should have companions and handmaidens, and I will bring them to you now."

At that Grace and Glory regarded him earnestly, and there were almost tears in her eyes, for she remembered Suffering and Sorrow, the faithful companions whom he had given her before. It had been through their help and gentleness and patience she had been able to ascend the mountains to the High Places. All the time she had been with her Lord and King, receiving her new name, and being crowned with joy and glory, she had been thinking of them and wishing—yes, actually wishing and longing that they were there too, for why should she receive everything? They had endured the same journey, had supported and helped her, had been through the same trials and attacks of the enemy.

Now she was here and they were not. She opened her mouth to make her first request, to beg her Lord to let her keep the companions he had chosen in the beginning and who had brought her to the glory of the High Places. Before she could speak, however, he said with the same specially lovely smile, "Here are the handmaidens, Grace and Glory, whom I have chosen to be with you henceforth and forever."

Two radiant, shining figures stepped forward, the morning sunshine glittering on their snowy garments, making them dazzling to look at. They were taller and stronger than Grace and Glory, but it was the beauty of their faces and the love shining in their eyes which caught at her heart and made her almost tremble with joy and admiration. They came toward her, their faces shining with mirth and gladness, but they said not a word.

"Who are you?" asked Grace and Glory softly. "Will you tell me your names?"

Instead of answering they looked at one another and smiled, then held out their hands as though to take hers in their own. At that familiar gesture, Grace and Glory knew them and cried out with a joy which was almost more than she could bear.

"Why! You are Suffering and Sorrow. Oh, welcome, welcome! I was longing to find you again."

They shook their heads. "Oh, no!" they laughed, "we are no more Suffering and Sorrow than you are Much-Afraid. Don't you know that everything that comes to the High Places is transformed? Since you brought us here with you, we returned into Joy and Peace."

"Brought you here!" gasped Grace and Glory. "What

an extraordinary way to express it! Why, from the first to last you dragged me here."

Again they shook their heads and smiled as they answered, "No, we could never have come here alone, Grace and Glory. Suffering and Sorrow may not enter the Kingdom of Love, but each time you accepted us and put your hands in ours we began to change. Had you turned back or rejected us, we never could have come here."

Looking at one another again, they laughed softly and said, "When first we saw you at the foot of the mountains, we felt a little depressed and despairing. You seemed so Much-Afraid of us, and shrank away and would not accept our help, and it looked so unlikely that any of us would ever get to the High Places. We told ourselves that we would have to remain Sorrow and Suffering always, but you see how graciously our Lord the King arranged for all of us, and you did bring us here. Now we are to be your companions and friends forever."

With that they came up to her, put their arms around her, and all three embraced and kissed one another with a love and thankfulness and joy beyond words to express. So with a new name, and united to the King and crowned with glory, Grace and Glory, accompanied by her companions and friends, came to the High Places and was led into the Kingdom of Love.

High Places

Grace and Glory with her handmaidens Joy and Peace stayed up on the High Places for several weeks while all three explored the heights and learned many new lessons from the King. He led them himself to many places, and explained to them as much as they were able to understand at that time. He also encouraged them to explore on their own, for there are always new and lovely discoveries to make up there on the High Places.

Even these High Places were not the highest of all. Others towered above them into the sky, where mortal eye could no longer follow them, and where only those who have finished their pilgrim life on earth are able to go. Grace and Glory and her friends were on the lowest, the "beginners' slopes" in the Kingdom of Love, and these were the parts which they were to explore and enjoy at this time. From these slopes, too, they were able to look down on the valleys below, and from that new viewpoint gain an understanding of many things which had been puzzling and mysterious to them before. From beneath they had not been seen clearly, and even then only a small part had been visible.

The first thing, however, which they realized up there on the slopes of the Kingdom of Love was how much more there would be to see and learn and understand when the King took them higher on future occasions. The glorious view which they now enjoyed was but small in comparison with all that lay beyond, and would be visible only from yet higher places above.

It was now perfectly evident to them that there must be ranges upon ranges of which they had never dreamed while they were still down in the narrow valleys with their extraordinarily limited views. Sometimes, as she looked on the glorious panorama visible from these lowest slopes in the Kingdom of Love, she found herself blushing as she remembered some of the dogmatic statements which she and others had made in the depths of the valley about the High Places and the ranges of Truth. They had been able to see so little and were so unconscious of what lay beyond

HIGH PLACES ❧ 119

and above. If that had been the case while down in the valley, how much more clearly, she now realized, that even up on those wonderful slopes she was only looking out on a tiny corner of the whole.

She never tired of looking from the glorious new viewpoint on the first slopes of the Kingdom of Love and seeing it all from a new perspective. What she could see and could take in almost intoxicated her with joy and thanksgiving, and sometimes even with inexpressible relief. Things which she had thought dark and terrible and which had made her tremble as she looked up from the Valley because they had seemed so alien to any part of the Realm of Love were now seen to be but parts of a great and wonderful whole. They were so altered and modified that as she saw what they extended into, she wondered at having been so blind and stupid at having had such false ideas about them.

She began to understand quite clearly that truth cannot be understood from books alone or by any written words, but only by personal growth and development in understanding, and that things written even in the Book of Books can be astonishingly misunderstood while one still lives on the low levels of spiritual experience and on the wrong side of the grave on the mountains.

She perceived that no one who finds herself up on the slopes of the Kingdom of Love can possibly dogmatize about what is seen there, because it is only then that she comprehends how small a part of the glorious whole she sees. All she can do is to gasp with wonder, awe, and thanksgiving, and to long with all her heart to go higher and to see and understand more.

Paradoxical as it may seem, as she gazed out on dazzling vistas, so glorious that she could not look at them steadily or grasp their magnificent sweep, she often thought that the prayer which best expressed her heart's desire was that of the blind man. "Lord, that I might receive my sight! Help me to open myself to more light. Help me to fuller understanding." Another thing which gave her continual joy was their unbroken communion with the King. Wherever he went she and Peace and Joy went too, springing behind him with a delight which at times was almost hilarious, for he was teaching and training them to use their hinds' feet. Grace and Glory quickly saw, however, that he always chose the way most carefully, and restrained his own amazing strength and power, taking only such spring and bounds as they could manage too.

So graciously did he adapt himself to what was possible to their newly acquired capacity that they scarcely recognized in the exhilaration of leaping and skipping like hinds on the mountains, that had he really extended his powers, they would have been left behind completely.

For Grace and Glory—who had been lame and limping all her life—the ecstasy of leaping about in this way and of bounding from rock to rock on the High Places as easily as the mountain roes, was so rapturous that she could hardly bear to cease from it even for rests. The King seemed to find great delight in encouraging this, and led her on and on, taking longer and longer leaps, until at last she would be quite breathless. Then as they sat side by side on some new crag to which he had led her, while she rested he would point out some of the vistas to be seen from the new viewpoint.

On one of these occasions after they had been up on the High Places for several days, she flung herself down on the lichen and moss-covered crag to which he had led her, and, laughing and breathless, said, "Even hinds' feet seem to need a rest now and then!"

"Grace and Glory," he answered, "do you think you

understand now how I was able to make your feet like hinds' feet and to set you on these High Places?"

She drew closer to him and looked earnestly in his face and asked, "How were you able to do this, my Lord and King?"

"Think back over the journey you made," he replied, "and tell me what lessons you learned on the way."

She was silent for a while as she reviewed the whole journey, which had seemed so terribly long and in some places so cruelly difficult and even impossible. She thought of the altars which she had built along the way; of the time when she had stood with him at the trysting-place in the Valley, when he had called her to follow him to the heights. She remembered the walk to the foot of the mountains; the first meeting with Suffering and Sorrow and of learning to accept their help; she recalled the shock of what had seemed such a heartbreaking detour down into the desert, and of the things which she had seen there.

Then their journey along the shores of Loneliness; the empty cove which the sea had filled to the brim; and then the agony of disappointment and frustration experienced in the wilderness when the path once again had turned away from the High Places. She remembered crossing the great sea-wall, walking through the woods and valleys until the rapturous moment when the path had turned back toward the mountains. Her thoughts turned to the Precipice of Injury, the Forests of Danger and Tribulation, the great storm during which they had sheltered in the hut. And then the mist—the endless mist, and the awful moment when the path suddenly led down into the Valley of Loss, and the nightmare abyss of horror into which she had looked when she had thought of turning back.

She recalled the descent down into the Valley of Loss and the peace she had found there before reascending to the heights in the aerial chairs, and of the days spent in that place where she had been prepared for her burial. Then that last agonizing ascent, and the cave where they sheltered from the floods and where she had been tempted to cast away the promises. Then the spring called Marah, and finally the mist-shrouded grave up among the peaks where she had been bound to the altar. How little she had imagined, when first she set out on that strange journey, what lay ahead of her and the things which she would be called upon to pass through. So for a long time she sat silent—remembering, wondering and thankful.

At last she put her hand in his and said softly, "My Lord, I will tell you what I learned."

"Tell me," he answered gently.

"First," said she, "I learned that I must accept with joy all that you allowed to happen to me on the way and everything to which the path led me! That I was never to try to evade it but to accept it and lay down my own will on the altar and say, 'Behold me, I am thy little handmaiden Acceptance-with-Joy.'"

He nodded without speaking, and she went on, "Then I learned that I must bear all that others were allowed to do against me and to forgive with no trace of bitterness and to say to thee, 'Behold me—I am thy little handmaiden Bearing-with-Love,' that I may receive power to bring good out of this evil."

Again he nodded, and she smiled still more sweetly and happily.

"The third thing that I learned was that you, my Lord, never regarded me as I actually was, lame and weak and crooked and cowardly. You saw me as I would be when you had done what you promised and had brought me to the High Places, when it could be truly said, 'There is none that walks with such a queenly ease, nor with such grace, as she.' You always treated me with the same love and graciousness as though I were a queen already and not wretched little Much-Afraid." Then she looked up into his face and for a little time could say no more, but at last she added, "My Lord, I cannot tell you how greatly I want to regard others in the same way."

A very lovely smile broke out on his face at that, but he still said nothing, only nodded for the third time and waited for her to continue.

"The fourth thing," said she with a radiant face, "was really the first I learned up here. Every circumstance in life, no matter how crooked and distorted and ugly it appears to be, if it is reacted to in love and forgiveness and obedience to your will can be transformed.

"Therefore I begin to think, my Lord, you purposely allow us to be brought into contact with the bad and evil things that you want changed. Perhaps that is the very reason why we are here in this world, where sin and sorrow and suffering and evil abound, so that we may let you teach us so to react to them, that out of them we can create lovely qualities to live forever. That is the only really satisfactory way of dealing with evil, not simply binding it so that it cannot work harm, but whenever possible overcoming it with good."

At last he spoke. "You have learned well, Grace and Glory. Now I will add one thing more. It was these lessons which you have learned which enabled me to change you from limping, crippled Much-Afraid into Grace and Glory with the hinds' feet. Now you are able to run, leaping on the mountains and able to follow me where I go, so that we need never be parted again.

"So remember this; as long as you are willing to be Acceptance-with-Joy and Bearing-in-Love, you can never again become crippled, and you will be able to go wherever I lead you. You will be able to go down into the Valley of the world to work with me there, for that is where the evil and sorrowful and ugly things are which need to be overcome.

"Accept and bear and obey the Law of Love, and nothing will be able to cripple your hinds' feet or to separate you from me. This is the secret of the High Places, Grace and Glory, it is the lovely and perfect law of the whole universe. It is this that makes the radiant joy of the Heavenly Places." Then he rose to his feet, drew her up beside him, and said, "Now use your hinds' feet again, for I am going to lead you to another part of the mountain."

Off he went, "leaping on the mountains and skipping on the hills," with Grace and Glory following close behind and the beautiful figures of Peace and Joy springing at her side. As they went she sang this song:

Set me as a seal upon thine heart
Thou Love more strong than death
That I may feel through every part
Thy burning, fiery breath.
And then like wax held in the flame,
May take the imprint of thy Name.
Set me a seal upon thine arm,
Thou Love that bursts the grave,
Thy coals of fire can never harm,
But only purge and save.
Thou jealous Love thou burning Flame,
Oh, burn out all unlike thy Name.
The floods can never drown thy Love,
Nor weaken thy desire,
The rains may deluge from above
But never quench thy fire.
Make soft my heart in thy strong flame,
To take the imprint of thy Name.

CANT. 8:6

Return to the Valley

THE PLACE TO WHICH the King of Love now brought them was a most beautiful valley among the peaks of the High Places. The whole of this sheltered spot was laid out in quiet gardens and orchards and vineyards. Here grew flowers of rarest beauty and lilies of every description. Here, too, were trees of spices and of many kinds of fruits, and nut trees, almonds and walnuts, and many other varieties which Grace and Glory had never seen before. Here the King's gardeners were always busy, pruning the trees, tending the plants and the vines, and preparing beds for new seedlings and tender shoots.

These the King himself transplanted from uncongenial soil and condition in the valleys below so that they might grow to perfection and bloom in that valley high above, ready to be planted in other parts of the Kingdom of Love, to beautify and adorn it where the king saw fit. They spent several delightful days watching the gardeners

as they worked under the gracious supervision of the King himself and accompanying him as he walked in the vineyards, teaching and advising those who tended the vines.

One day, however, Grace and Glory with her two attendants walked to the end of the valley and found themselves on the very edge of the High Places, from which they could look right down into the Low Places far below. As they stood there they saw a long, green valley between two chains of mountains through which a river wound like a ribbon of light. Here and there were patches of brown and red which seemed to be villages and dwelling places, surrounded with trees and gardens.

All of a sudden, Grace and Glory gave a queer little gasp, for she recognized the place. They were looking down into the Valley of Humiliation itself, the place where she had lived in misery for so long and from which the Shepherd had called her to the High Places.

Without a word she sat down on the grassy slope, and

as she looked a multitude of thoughts filled her mind. Down there was the little white cottage where she had lived, and the pastures where the shepherds tended the King's flocks. There were the sheepfolds, and the stream where the flocks went to drink and where she had met the Shepherd for the first time. In that valley were all her fellow workers and the friends among whom she had lived and with whom she had enjoyed such happy fellowship.

Others she had known were there, too. Away on the outskirts of the village was the cottage where her Aunt Dismal Forebodings lived and where she had spent her miserable childhood with her cousins Gloomy and Spiteful and Craven Fear. As she thought of them and their wretched existence a pang of compassion and pain shot through her heart.

Poor Aunt Dismal, trying to hide the fact that her heart was broken by the unhappy marriages which her two daughters had made, and embittered by the shameful doings of her darling son. She saw the dwellings of her other relatives; the Manor House, where decrepit old Lord Fearing lived, tortured by his failing powers and his dread of approaching death. There was the house where Pride lived, and near it the homes of Bitterness and Resentment, and under those dark trees lived miserable Self-Pity. She recognized the dwelling places of those who had so harassed her on her journey to the High Places, and round about were the homes of other inhabitants of the Valley, people who hated or despised or rejected the Shepherd.

As Grace and Glory sat looking down into the Valley the tears welled into her eyes and her heart throbbed with pain, two sensations which she had completely forgotten up there on the High Places.

Suddenly she discovered that her feelings toward her relatives and those who lived down there in the Valley had undergone a complete change, and she saw them in a new light. She had thought of them only as horrible enemies, but now she realized that they were just miserable beings such as she had been herself. They were indwelt and tormented by their different besetting sins and ugly natures, just as she had been by her fears. They were wretched slaves to the natures which gave them their names, and the more horrible the qualities which characterized them, the more misery they endured, and the more we should show them compassion.

She could scarcely bear the thought, yet for so many years she had not only feared but also condemned them, had actually "disdained their misery," telling herself it was their own fault. Yes, she, detestable, fear-enslaved Much-Afraid had actually dared to disdain them for the things which made them so wretched and ugly when she herself was equally wretched and enslaved. Instead of a fellow feeling of compassion and passionate desire that they might be delivered and transformed from the pride and resentment and bitterness which made them what they were, she had just detested and despised them.

When she thought of that she turned to Joy and Peace, who were sitting beside her, and cried out desperately, "Can nothing be done for them down there in the Valley? Must my Aunt Dismal be left unhelped, and poor Spiteful and Gloomy too, and those cousins who went so far with us on the way to the High Places, trying to turn us back! If the Shepherd could deliver me, Grace and Glory, from all my fears and sins, couldn't he deliver them also from the things which torment them?"

"Yes," said Joy (who had been Sorrow). "If he can turn Sorrow into Joy, Suffering into Peace, and Much-Afraid into Grace and Glory, how can we doubt that he could change Pride and Bitterness and Resentment and Self-Pity too, if they would but yield to him and follow him?

And your Aunt Dismal could be changed into Praise and Thanksgiving, and poor Gloomy and Spiteful also. We cannot doubt that it could be done that they could be completely delivered from all the things which torment them."

"But," cried Grace and Glory, "how can they be persuaded to follow the Shepherd? At present they hate him and won't go near him."

Then Peace (who before had been Suffering) said quietly, "I have noticed that when people are brought into sorrow and suffering, or loss, or humiliation, or grief, or into some place of great need, they sometimes become ready to know the Shepherd and to seek his help. We know, for example, that your Aunt Dismal is desperately unhappy over the behavior of poor Craven Fear, and it may be that she would be ready now to turn to the Shepherd. Then poor Gloomy and Spiteful are so wretched that though they felt no need of the Shepherd before, it is very possible that now is the time to try to persuade them to seek his help."

"Yes!" exclaimed Grace and Glory, "I am sure you are right. Oh, if only we could go to them! If only there were some way of helping them to find what we have found."

At that very moment, close at hand, sounded the voice of the King. He came and sat down beside them, looked with them down into the Valley so far below, and said gently to Grace and Glory, "Thou that dwellest in the gardens, the companions hearken to thy voice; cause me to hear it" (Cant. 8:13).

Grace and Glory turned to him and laid her hand upon his arm. "My Lord," she said, "we were talking about the people who live down there in the Valley of Humiliation. There are my relatives, you know, all of them. They are so wretched and miserable. What can we do for them, my Lord? They don't know anything about the joy of the High Places and the Kingdom of Love. There is my poor Aunt Dismal Forebodings. I lived with her for a long time, and know that she is utterly wretched."

"I know her," said the King quietly, "she is a most unhappy woman."

"And her daughter Gloomy," went on Grace and Glory, looking at him entreatingly as she spoke. "She married Coward, the son of old Lord Fearing, very rich, but much older than herself and a miserably unhappy and selfish creature. I believe she has not known a moment's peace since. There was talk in the Valley before I came away, that he was likely to desert her."

"He has done so," answered the King quietly, "and she

has returned to her mother in the cottage, a miserable and disillusioned woman with a broken heart."

"And her sister Spiteful. Poor, poor soul, with her sharp tongue which makes so many enemies and deprives her of friends. She married Timid-Skulking, and they are desperately poor, and have to live in one little rented room in the house of my cousin Bitterness and his wife. I cannot bear to think of their wretched condition while I live up here in the Kingdom of Love."

"They are wretched indeed," said the King, even more gently and compassionately than before. "They have just lost the little daughter who poor Spiteful had hoped would be such a comfort to them in their dreary circumstances."

"And then," continued Grace and Glory with just a

hint of hesitation in her voice, "there is their brother Craven Fear." She did not look at the King as she spoke, but paused a moment, then went on hurriedly. "He is the most unhappy member of the whole family. He has broken his mother's heart; neither of his sisters will speak to him any more, and he goes skulking about the Valley hated by everyone."

"I know him," replied the King gravely, but with just a hint of a smile. "I know him well. You do not exaggerate when you speak of his wretchedness. I have had to interfere and chastise him many times to try and correct his bullying propensities. But 'though I have chastened him sore I have not given him over unto death.'"

"No, no!" cried Grace and Glory imploringly, "don't ever do that, My Lord! Oh, I beg you, find some way to rescue and deliver him from himself, as you delivered me."

He made no answer for a little while, only looked at her very kindly and with a look of great contentment and happiness on his face. At last he spoke. "I am more than willing to do what you suggest," said he. "But, Grace and Glory, these unhappy souls we are speaking about will not allow me into their homes, nor even permit me to speak to them. I need a voice to speak for me, to persuade them to let me help them."

"I see what you mean," she cried joyfully. "We will go down with you and speak to them and show what you have done for us and what you are willing and able to do for them."

"Do you think they will listen to you?" he asked, smiling at her very gently as he spoke.

"No, I don't think it's at all likely—at least, not at first," she answered. "I was not at all the sort of person to make them want to listen to me. I did not behave at all lovingly to them, but you will tell me what to say. You will teach me and I will say it for you.

"O my Lord, let us make haste, and go down there. When they see what you have done for me, when they see Peace and Joy, I do think in the end they will want you to help them too. It is because they have lied to themselves about you and have persuaded themselves that you cannot do them good that they resist you and turn from your help, but we will plead with them. Especially now, my Lord, when they are so unhappy and so despised by others. Their very misery and loneliness and sorrow will make them more willing to listen to news of your grace and of your desire to help them."

"True," he agreed, "that is just what I think. This is indeed a specially favorable time for us to go down and try to help them."

He rose to his feet as he spoke. She sprang up too, and all four stood joyful and radiant on the edge of the High Places, ready to go leaping down to the Valley again. Then Grace and Glory saw that the great waterfall quite close at hand was leaping down to the Valley too, with the tumultuous, joyful noise of many waters, singing as they poured themselves down over the rock lip.

From the heights we leap and flow
To the valleys down below,
Sweetest urge and sweetest will.
To go lower, lower still.

Suddenly she understood. She was beholding a wondrous and glorious truth; "a great multitude whom no man could number: brought like herself by the King to the Kingdom of Love and to the High Places so that they could now pour out their lives in gladdest abandonment, leaping down with him to the sorrowful, desolate places below, to share with others the life which they had received. She herself was only one drop among that glad, exultant throng of Self-givers, the followers of the King of Love, united with him and with one another, each one equally blessed and beloved as herself. "For he loves each one of us," she said to herself, "as though there were only one to love."

The thought of being made one with the great fall of many waters filled her heart with ecstasy and with a rapturous joy beyond power to express. She, too, at last, was to go down with them, pouring herself forth in Love's abandonment of Self-giving. "He brought me to the heights just for this," she whispered to herself, and then looked at him and nodded.

At that he began leaping and springing down the mountainside before them, bounding from rock to rock, always choosing, however, leaps which were within their power to follow, and sure footholds for less experienced feet. Behind him went Grace and Glory, with Joy and Peace beside her, leaping down, just as the waters leaped and sang beside them. They mingled their voices with the joyful music of the many waters, singing their own individual song:

Make haste, Beloved, be thou like an hart
On mountains spicy sweet:
And I, on those High Places where thou art,
Will follow on hinds' feet;
As close behind the hart, there leaps the roe,
So where thou goest, I will surely go.

That, as perhaps you know, is the last verse of the Song of Songs, which is Solomon's. But for Grace and Glory it was the beginning of a new song altogether.

Lessons Learned on the Slopes of the High Places

WRITTEN DURING A THREE-WEEK visit to Switzerland on my way back to Israel after a short visit to England following the death of my father and the winding up of his affairs. I had said farewell, as I thought, to the old home in which I had been born and where I had been welcomed back by my father on all my furloughs from missionary work in the Middle East.

Come Up to Me into the Mount

BRAUNWALD MONDAY, MAY 23, 1949

"And the LORD said . . . , Come up to me into the mount. . . . And a *cloud* covered the *mount*. And the glory of the LORD abode upon [the] *mount* . . . and the *cloud* covered it six days: and the seventh day he called unto Moses out of the midst of the *cloud*. . . . And the LORD spake" (Ex. 24:12, 15-16; 25:1).

Through mist and cloud and by a strange path where I could never see more than one step at a time, the Lord has brought me here to Switzerland, "to a high mountain apart." I believe that he will speak to me out of the cloud; for I know he has something to say, and I long to hear it.

Three days ago as I came up in the funicular railway from Linthal to Braunwald, in Glarus, there was such thick mist and cloud that nothing at all was visible. Not a chalet nor tree nor wall could be seen, and even the Bergfrieden Deaconess House was quite invisible until we reached the door!

The sisters said that for over a week it had been very like that, and it might continue in the same way for weeks longer. Humanly speaking, it was very disappointing to come to Switzerland after so many years' absence, and be unable to see anything.

But that evening from my window in the huge wooden chalet I saw one patch of rocky precipice and snow exposed for a few moments through the driving rain and mist. I had been told that the snow mountains rise in a glorious range just the other side of the valley, but I could never have guessed so from what was visible.

Next morning I awoke at 4:30 a.m., and there the mountains were! How right those people are who say that one might just as well not come to Switzerland unless one is prepared to rise before the sun! Now the mountains appeared. Still lying in bed, I saw them through the uncurtained window—their tops still buried in the cloud—but a glorious snow and rock range rising like a wall just across the narrow valley. All that day the mist was clearing, but the *clouds* remained low and still hid most of the view.

Today I awoke at 5:00 a.m., and lo! Clear and rosy in the dawn light against a background of calm blue sky were the High Places I so longed to see.

Now I am sitting on a huge green slope starred with tiny blue gentians, and the buttercups are scattered like gold all around me. This is the Braunwald Alp, and the snow mountains rise like walls on three sides of it. I sit here and look out on beauty beyond expression. To the right is an immense cliff over which the Brumbach waterfall leaps down with a noise "of many waters." Opposite me is a mountain with huge rock walls and seven peaks rising one above the other. Beside them, though not quite so high, is another peak shaped like a horn. This seven-crested mountain is the Ortstock and the horn is called Hoher Turm. This is the mountain that dominates the scene in Braunwald, and it is more picturesque than any of the other neighboring giants.

To the left rise great ramparts and ranges of snow and rock. While I sit here in brilliant sunshine, an immense dark cloud has overshadowed the heights, and I hear a distant peal of thunder. So through cloud and mist I have come to the place on the Mount where I believe the Lord is going to speak to me, and reveal the reason why he has brought me back to the beloved Swiss mountains after an absence of so many years!

The Brumbach Falls

The whole neighborhood is filled with the sound of rushing water pouring down over and between the rocks. For me, the two falls, the Brumbach and the Zillbach, are like two glorious angels of love, leaping down from the heights to carry life and power to the valleys far below.

O my Lord! What do you want to say to me today? Help me to hear your voice. Teach me to understand the language spoken by your creation all around me. Help me to receive into my innermost soul the great truth that, "To whom much is given, of them shall much be required."

Lifting my eyes, I look across the valley at the Brumbach falls and see the water pouring itself down in an extraordinary ecstasy of self-abandoned giving—and I know now that is my Lord's message to me.

I have asked him to help me to understand the language of this book of nature. And the first message and lesson his creation utters is this one. It is so clear that I do understand it. It speaks of love's eternal ecstatic joy in ceaseless, blissful giving.

1. The first characteristic of true love is *humility:* the pouring of oneself down lower and lower in self-effacement and self-denial. The message of running water always is, "Go lower. Find the lowest place. That is the only way to true fulfillment."

2. The next characteristic of love is *giving.* The poured-out life

gives life and power to others. The more love gives, the more it fulfills itself. "For it is Love's prerogative to GIVE and GIVE and GIVE."

3. The third characteristic of love is *service.* The Brumbach falls, in the act of giving themselves, serve the whole valley and far beyond it. The water means a supply of irrigation, electricity, and light for many, many homes, gardens, and orchards. To be utterly abandoned to the goal of giving oneself to others, and going down lower, is the joy and ecstasy of love.

"Perfect love casteth out fear." Yes, that is what the water utters so exultingly as it rushes toward the great, terrifying rocky lip of the gorge and plunges over, utterly abandoned and unafraid of the dreadful depths into which it must fall, down onto the threatening rocks below.

Watching the waters as they leap over the edge, and following them with my eyes as they fall downward, I discover that the whole movement is one of the most breathtaking examples of utter rejoicing and of triumphant, almost delirious abandonment that I have ever seen. If one looks at the falls as a whole, they are marvelously beautiful. But if one gazes at one particular part of the water as it plunges over the lip, and then watches it as it falls right down, the almost crazy, blissful abandonment is staggering. I never saw motion so utterly expressive of joy! The movement looks like perfect rapture, fearless surrender to a hitherto unknown delight, the greatest it is possible to experience. The downward motion is light, adventurous, and perfectly happy. The water, after casting itself over the rocks, seems to be held up and supported as though floating down on wings! A glorious contradiction indeed.

How can one abandon oneself in this way? Well, the scene before me answers this question.

The falls come down from the *heights.* Before they can do that there must first come the experience of "He maketh my feet like hinds' feet, and setteth me upon my high places" (Psa. 18:33).

One cannot get a mighty and powerful *fall* of water if there is only a low place and a short way for it to fall. It is the "high places" of faith and obedience which make the falls of love possible!

The Ortstock, the great seven-pinnacled mountain opposite, is a wonderful picture of spiritual experience, rising from height to height and peak to peak. The summits of the "high places" are the powerhouses from which love pours itself down in joyful surrender. One can never truly love until by faith and surrendered obedience one reaches the "high places" and there learns to go "skipping and leaping" on the mountains of difficulty as though there were "an asphalt road"!

Everything around me seems to be designed to emphasize this lesson. I have been brought to a place where all God's creation appears to be uttering things in a language which only become clearly audible and understood by hearts that have been learning in the school of suffering. It is the language which one begins to spell out in one's innermost soul when one is on a cross to which self is being transfixed by nails of pain and anguish of heart. It compares to the experiences in the Siege of Jerusalem, and the years in terrorist-ridden Palestine which led up to this past year, 1948.

Have I not been brought here to experience some great re-adjustment in my spiritual nature? Instinctively the old nature at once cries out, "Oh, will it be very painful? Hasn't there been enough of it already, dear Lord Jesus?" And then I laugh. Shall the clay vessel on the Lord's wheel and under his loving, molding hands, think of pain in the last stage of a long, joyous yielding to his patient fashioning? The only thing that matters is that the adjustment of abandonment to selfless love be made perfectly, so that I stop seeking to be loved and abandon myself to the joy of giving love to others.

How beautifully someone has summed this up in the words of an old Quaker lady quoted to me, "Self-sacrifice is the ecstasy of giving the best we have to the one we love the most."

The sound of falling water and the bells of the cows as they graze on the mountain slopes are the only things audible in this quiet valley. But the sound of the water is continuous—it never stops. It is saying over and over again, "The secret of experiencing true love is to go lower. Pour yourself down, Go lower and lower. Give and give and give, and serve with joyful abandonment." O my Lord! How I thank you!

The Sesselbahn

BRAUNWALD MAY 24, 1949

Yesterday morning the Lord was teaching me the most fascinating lesson from the Sesselbahn.

High above Braunwald, on the slopes of Eggstocke, is the Ortstock Haus. It stands near a great precipice and it is connected with Braunwald, far beneath it, by the Sesselbahn—a system of overhead cables slung from lofty pylons fixed in the rocky slopes of the mountain. On these cables, cars are hung which are electrically caused to slide up the cables carrying provisions to the Ortstock Haus.

As I climbed the gentian-starred slopes to my usual prayer and trysting place with the Lord, I could hear the lines beginning to ring overhead, and I kept waiting to see the cars that would go swinging up those aerial lines to the heights far above. I was told that people, as well as cartons of provisions, could ascend in them.

At last, at the end of the morning, I saw the aerial vehicle and got a shock! It was not a walled-in car which came rolling down the cable, but just two chairs—similar to ordinary metal garden ones, with a kind of sunshade cover fixed over them. There was no protection of any kind, just two chairs dangling in the air, side by side. In one of the chairs a solitary man was sitting, with nothing underneath him but a narrow footrest fixed to the bottom of the chair. Apparently he had been up the line testing the cables.

In the evening as I walked to the Braunwald Alp through a pine wood, I could see and hear that the Sesselbahn was in full swing. One after another these fragile, completely unenclosed chairs went running up the cables, swinging over fearsome abysses and up the face of a mighty rock precipice. One after another, up they went, and down they came in a never-ending chain. At first I thought that ever so many people must be going up in them. And then, as I could see no one, I thought they must be empty. But on the way home I passed the lower terminus or station, and saw the chairs swinging into the station shed, all of them quite empty. Then they reemerged a few minutes later with small boxes and crates strapped onto them. A never-ending chain of supplies was going up to the house on the heights, ready for the expected tourist visitors who, as soon as the mists cleared, would start making the ascent.

It seemed to me then, that the Sesselbahn was one of the loveliest and most fascinating pictures of faith imaginable. For faith has nothing to do with intellectual belief. *Faith is obedience.* Faith and abandonment to God's will and power are inseparable.

Faith is willingness to do God's will. Unwillingness to abandon one's own will and to obey God is unbelief.

There they were, those tiny chairs with no sides or backs—only a couple of bars. The cable by whose power they traveled overhead, and at great distance, was quite invisible. Underneath there was nothing but the abyss, and no earthly ground of support. All one saw was two moving chairs, apparently hanging in the air. But they were supported—from above! The power came from above, and by means of that power they were able to travel upward, in defiance of the law of gravity. They went higher and higher, fixed with a wheel which ran up one cable and down another.

One had only to be willing to trust the invisible power, sit down on a chair, and abandon oneself completely. No self-effort was possible. Then one would be wafted upward to the heights. It was all a matter of faith and no works—except for the initial work of choosing to abandon oneself to the Sesselbahn. But, oh, how terrifying that choice looked to me! I am so wary of heights and afraid that panic will send me crazily throwing myself down from the pinnacle. It is a fear that has assailed me all my life and kept me from climbing high mountains as other members of the family loved to do. What if the cable broke or the power failed? Nothing beneath except broken bones or death. No earthly support!

I could only too readily imagine that any nervous person or someone afraid of heights would be appalled at the very thought of such a journey. True, there would be nothing to do but rest in the chair and be carried upward. But, oh! How easy to get in a panic and fall.

How like that overhead cable the promises of God often seem to be. They look so appallingly frail and unsafe and without earthly support of any kind, apparently leading to such impossible situations. It seems they certainly cannot be relied upon, for we tell ourselves how easily we may be mistaken and claim what was never meant for us personally, but only for great courageous saints of God, prophets, and apostles.

But once we abandon ourselves to these promises, and enter into them in the abandonment of faith and obedience, then all the overhead power begins to work. The traveler resting on and in the promise does nothing but remain in it. Having trusted the promise enough to risk everything upon it, up one goes! And no power on earth can hinder arrival at the consummation of the promise and its perfect fulfillment. Though we may seem to meet the most horrifying precipices confronting us, and abysses far below which we could never hope to ascend nor pass over in our own strength, yet in the spiritual Sesselbahn of faith and obedience, everything is triumphantly surmounted.

For an hour I watched quite fascinated, for my path led up the valley high over which the chairs went swinging on their way to the heights above. And my Lord spoke to me and said:

"God is not a man, that he should lie . . . hath he said,
and shall he not do it? Or hath he spoken, and shall he

not make it good?" (Num. 23:19). Fear not to journey on
to all the tests and threatening difficulties in the area to
which you are returning. As I was with you in the Siege
of Jerusalem, and though you think that you now have no
home to which to return in England, yet I will be with
you everywhere I lead you and in every circumstance in
which you find yourself.

Oh, yes! One may catch one's breath as one begins the challenging ascent in one of his promises, looking forward to what seems an awfully dangerous precipice. One may feel dizzy as one is swung across and over an abyss between two peaks. But the promises are sure; and trustfully sitting in them, one goes running up to greater things.

The Torrent

BRAUNWALD MAY 25, 1949

Today I started to walk to the Riet Alp. There was lovely sunshine and I made my way down through the fields rejoicing in all the beauty. The fields were golden with the most beautiful kingcups and dandelions, and tiny gentians like blue gems were everywhere. The Brumbach and the Zillbach falls faced me. I walked rejoicing as though in heaven, awed at the way all nature around me was sounding forth the utterances of God.

Ever since going through the Siege of Jerusalem in 1948 and being in constant danger of death, it seems that my physical senses have been quickened to enjoy the beauties, scents, and sounds of nature to a far higher degree than before. That is part of the legacy of joy and blessing which those terrifying experiences bestowed upon me.

In the old days when I visited Switzerland as a girl, I used to be thrilled by the beauties of nature in a special way: I loved the scent of the pine woods, of the damp cones and needles carpeting the ground; the sawn logs and moss- and lichen-covered rocks. But now it all means unutterably more to me. I find nature a book of marvels, the language of which I have just begun to understand and interpret. So I walked in ecstasy, with natural beauties around me speaking forth the praises and character of the Creator. Everything uttered his name.

I came to the sawmill beside the torrent which runs down the valley from the foot of the Brumbach falls. The water which I saw rushing so blithely over and among the rocks, and under the bridge, was the same water which, high overhead, had come to a great crisis and leaped so exultantly and with such blissful abandonment over the falls.

I stood on the bridge and looked at it. Yesterday I had asked myself, "What does the water do when, after its magnificent abandoned leap, it reaches the cruel rocks below, and there is no longer the ecstasy of leaping down, only a rough, rock-obstructed everyday course before it?"

On the bridge I saw, and laughed to see, what happens to the water. The bed of the torrent was strewn with huge rocks. There were obstructions everywhere. But the water came rushing along, laughing and rejoicing and absolutely delighted to find its way over and around all the obstacles and difficulties. It seemed as happy and cheerful forcing its way among the trim rocks as when it threw itself down over the heights.

What a lesson I learned as I watched it: I think almost the loveliest of all of them. Day after day, once the leap of obedience has been made, the power of the waters following along behind, added to the steepness of the riverbed, makes the surmounting of difficulties and obstacles—of every kind—a daily delight.

Then the meadows of flowers added their lovely voices emphasizing the message of the rushing waters. They were so small and yet so brilliant. There were so many of them carpeting the fields, and apart from their beauty, in a way so unnecessary! I asked the Lord to help me to understand the message he wanted them to give me, and they simply chuckled and sang it to me.

We are all our Creator God's extra loving-kindnesses and tender mercies. We blossom beside the paths of obedience, and all over the fields of life. He makes us flourish to give delight to anyone who may see us. Some people take us for granted, as though we are so common and ordinary that it is not worthwhile noticing us. They see no beauty to cause delight. But every worshiping, grateful soul thrills with awe and delight and wonder at the daily blessings and loving-kindnesses of the Creator Father.

The Haustock and the Gentians

I walked perhaps for three quarters of an hour, to a place where the Ortstock mountain was behind me, and I seemed to be in a completely different environment. The seven peaks no longer dominated the scene. Instead, the Riet Alp lay ahead, and all the other snow mountains were seen from a completely different angle.

For the first time since my arrival the clouds rose so high, that for a few minutes I was even able to see the Haustock rising 3,160 meters high. There it was, straight before me, the second highest mountain of the whole range—only cloud-hidden Todi being higher. It was also the whitest of them all. It rose up like a tremendous pyramid, and its triangular summit seemed to be walled off by a gigantic, perfectly smooth wall of rock on which the snow could not rest. It stretched across the whole peak.

It filled me with the new thrill as it spoke forth a new lesson, reminding me of the great and astonishing differences there are in the lives and circumstances of people everywhere around the world.

For example: The Ortstock which dominates the scene from Braunwald is far and away the most picturesque mountain in sight. With its seven rocky peaks rising one above the other, it beckons to higher places all the time. It is my special mountain! I love it, for somehow it seems to picture my own adventurous, and in some ways out of the ordinary, kind of life. Constantly I have been challenged to new adventures and leaps to new heights of faith. Moreover, the Brumbach and the Zillbach falls leap down the mountains' sides. But as the people at the table in the pension house remarked, "The Ortstock is the most picturesque and perhaps the most spectacular of the group of mountains, but it does not rise to such heights as do many of the others."

Yes, there are some lives that tower up to far sublimer heights than others which may appear more showy and spectacular. My beloved Ortstock does not soar so very high, beautiful though it is. It came to me with great comfort and peace, as I walked along the path, that privileged and unusual as my lot is—to live and work in Jerusalem at the time of Israel's return to the ancient Homeland—yet I am still "very small fry"! The task I am called to is small compared to others, though my life is adventurous and exciting. But there are other lives in circumstances much less picturesque to look at, which tower sublimely up like the Haustock, to far greater heights of obedience and faith and self-surrender. They may appear to have very uneventful slopes and no outstanding peaks until the summit is reached. But, oh, how majestically they show forth their Lord's glory when that summit is reached!

After a brief, breathless scramble I came to the Riet Alp slopes where the cow chalets are. By then a fine rain had started to fall. How sudden the changes of weather are out here. I find no one bold enough to forecast whether it will be fine or not. I gathered some of the huge gentians which grow on the Riet Alp and then sought shelter under the eaves of a cowshed and hoped for the rain to stop. But soon it was clear that the clouds were descending in every direction and there was no hope that the rain would end. I hurried down the steep track before the rain would make it dangerously slippery. Then for an hour I walked home through a steady, persistent downpour.

The temptation came to repine and resent the rain and to long for the sunshine. But I remembered the message given me by dear friends who had met me at the Zurich airport: "Go through each day praising and thanking God for everything that happens!" Nothing can take from me the memories and beauties and lessons of these three days. So I praised as I walked through the steady downpour, and soon I found that the rain and the clouds and the mist were also sounding forth messages from my Lord.

How suddenly the change had come. One moment I was gazing almost breathlessly at the beauty of the Haustock as the clouds lifted from it for the first time. Then just half an hour later all the snow mountains were blotted out as completely as if they did not exist. Before I got back to the Bergfrieden Pension Haus all the nearer hills and fields and chalets had disappeared, and mist and rain completely shrouded the landscape. Then my Lord said, "These changes come in life, too. For one hour the vision on the Mount, and then perhaps, almost directly, the descent into the depths of the valley where the vision may seem to be completely blotted out by changed circumstances. But believe steadfastly in what I showed you in the hours of vision and clear sky. The reality is there still, even though a curtain seems to blot it out. You *have* seen the Haustock, and though there is no trace of it now, and it has disappeared like a dream, nevertheless it is there. It is a reality. But the mist and cloud are transient and will pass away, and the true reality appear again!"

A lovely message indeed, even though the feeling was a rather miserable one of extreme wetness! I reached the Pension House sopping wet, changed into a new outfit of dry clothes, and verily the Riet Alp did seem to have disappeared as though out of existence.

But there in a vase on my table were the gentians which I had picked on its slopes. I may not be able to show anyone the Riet Alp at present, nor the vision that God gave me yesterday—but the Riet Alp is certainly there, as my gentians testify. And the purposes and plans which God showed me, and his pattern, also remain true. These little notebooks with their records of what he made me see are like the gentians, a visible testimony to the eye of faith!

Ascension Day: Ascent to the Highest

BRAUNWALD 7:20 A.M.

Now it is all breathtakingly beautiful, although when I awoke it was cloudier than ever, and my precious two weeks are nearly half finished already. But as I lie on the bed the great snow peaks opposite are all shining in the morning light and the sky is blue. The clouds are no longer gray and heavy, but are white and fluffy. The cowbells are tinkling, the sun is shining, and now the Deaconess sisters are going from room to room singing Ascension Day hymns. They have just stood at my bedroom door and sung (of course, in Swiss German).

"Now we sing with the great multitude, ALLELUIA."

Oh, yes, Lord Jesus. Amen! This morning everything is uttering forth your praise, as the mist upon the peaks rolls away and the light is like the shining of your face!

"And Moses went up into the mount . . . and the *cloud* covered it six days: and the *seventh* day he called unto Moses out of the midst of the *cloud*" (Ex. 24:15-16).

It is the seventh day since my arrival and the first perfectly fine one. The mountains stand out clearly against a cloudless blue sky. As I came down the slopes of the Braunwald Alp from my special trysting place with the loving Lord, the Sesselbahn chairs came swinging down the overhead cables one after the other. And there, to my consternation, laughing and gesticulating excitedly over my head, were ever so many of the Bergfrieden sisters. The lady who sits at the same table with me was also there. She had said she would go with me up to the Echstock that afternoon if it were fine. But evidently I had left the house too early to hear of the change of plans, and they had all gone up that morning without me. I had been left behind. So if I wanted to go up in those terrifying Sesselbahn chairs which so fascinated me, I must venture in them alone!

Once again a great temptation to feel disappointed leaped at me: And then I found myself praising the Lord and deciding to go alone! Yes, I, who am so afraid of heights and cannot persuade myself even to go up a church tower, or look out of a high-storied building, and who had been so horrified at the first sight of the aerial chairs, was now actually longing to go and to be carried up to the heights in a dizzy-looking dangling seat.

So after lunch I hurried off to the Sesselbahn station. I was afraid of being afraid, but a strange, exultant urge was upon me—for the Sesselbahn as a picture of God's promises had been such an inspiration to me these last few days that I felt I must trust myself to it in actual fact, almost as an outward sign of my inner surrender to God's future plans and purposes.

When I got to the station a real shock awaited me. The man said that something had gone wrong with the electric cable at the top of the mountain and they were going to stop the ascent and descent of the chairs. But if I liked, I could go up when the last people got down, in a short time, and then wait up on the heights while the cable was put right.

Even the news that the cable was not in order could not deter me, for I was so afraid that it would rain again the next day. But when I found that no one else was going up, and I would be swinging there in the chairs all alone, it did make me falter. Six Swiss women had just come along and looked at the chairs and the cable and the heights. They said they were afraid to go, and advised me not to go either. I too turned and started to go away, but the man ran after me and said that the chairs were just coming down. So I went back and waited. Then another woman and a girl came along and said they would make the ascent too.

At 2:24 p.m. we stepped into the chairs! As there were only three of us going up, and the woman and the girl were together in one pair of chairs, I was put in the first pair with an empty seat beside me. I was all alone!

The workman who was to repair the line in the station on the peak had been swung off first. Quite a wide space is left between each pair of chairs. I sat and watched him start off and waited for my turn. My heart beat rather tumultuously, but I was astonished to find how calm I felt. I had told myself that I, who was so terrified of heights and big drops, could not possibly go in the Sesselbahn. Yet here I was—without a companion to talk to me and reassure me and put a protecting hand over my arm—sitting in the chair and waiting to be swung off toward the high places. The whole thing had now become a symbol of the abandonment of faith, and I could not turn back.

The station attendant grinned at me; the girl in the chair behind me giggled nervously, and they all cried out, *"Auf Wiedersehen!"* ("Good-bye till we meet again!") Then the man pulled a handle and my chair ran forward outside the station. For the next fifteen minutes I would be able to do nothing to stop or prevent myself from being swung high in the air and up and over a terrifying-looking precipice. There was nothing I could do even if I panicked. There I must sit or throw myself out of the seat.

The chairs simply shoot out from the station at great speed, I suppose in order to get a good upward swing like an airplane rushing along the ground just before takeoff. But once outside and high on the line, the running is beautifully smooth and steady.

It was wonderful. The green slopes beneath were gold and blue with buttercups and gentians, and snow peaks towered all around. Going up the line, the chairs do not face the precipice but look out on the mountains of the other side of the valley. Coming down, one faces the Ortstock and the Echstock and its great precipice.

Up and up we went, and the height did not seem dreadful at all. Just for one moment, after swinging over my usual prayer place and reaching the ravine with its huge jagged rocks, I did feel a slightly odd feeling which I knew if I gave way to it would lead to real panic. The thought, *Oh I can't stop and get out even if I want to*, sprang into my mind. I gripped the armrest and gasped, "The Lord is my shepherd. . . . I will fear no evil: for thou art with me" (Psa. 23). Then the feeling of panic passed instantly, and from that moment I was swung upward almost in an ecstasy of delight, as the marvelously beautiful views opened before me. The valleys and slopes were left behind and the mountains were all around—their peaks drawing nearer and nearer.

I could see the chairs with the woman and girl coming up some distance behind me. My back was to the precipice and my face was toward the peaks. Then the precipice was actually underneath and there were higher green, flower-covered slopes. Yet still we ran up and up, and then the terminus actually became visible. With a rattle, my chair dipped and ran into a long, dark shed, and a man, looking rather surprised to see a woman quite alone, pulled the chairs to a standstill and I stepped out. The overhead power had carried me to the top.

On the High Places of the Echstock

Leaving the shed, I took a narrow path up a high green slope, till I came to the shoulder of the Echstock. There were wide patches of snow and no trees anywhere. Twenty minutes of steep walking brought me to the top, and even the station where I had left the chairs now seemed far below. I panted up the last part of the way, to the very foot of the steep rock pinnacle, and so arrived at the place where the Lord wanted to bring me.

I realized immediately as I stood there and looked all around, that this was, quite literally, the seventh day, and that God was going to speak to me in quite a special way. That was why he had called me up there alone, and not with the group who had gone up in the morning. Now I had two hours to spend alone with him on the high places.

I sat down on the springy moss and turf. The cold breeze, which had been apparent while we were rising, had now died down. The sun shone brilliantly and warmly. So for two hours I sat there and listened to him speaking.

His call came to me and the message of the Sesselbahn also became utterly clear.

I know that what he has called me to, he will enable me to do. "Faithful is he that calleth you, who also will do it" (1 Thess. 5:24).

The shoulder of the Echstock is like a wall and watershed, dividing two valleys. From this green seat I now looked out on a sister valley which was also surrounded by snow peaks. Up there it was as though I sat on a throne "high and lifted up," as it were, on a stool at the feet of God.

The "still small voice" spoke and said, "Hannah, build me here an altar."

This time there was no struggle, no shrinking dread, no anguish of surrender, only joy and love, and awe and hope and worship. A deep silent delight filled my heart as I realized that the way had been prepared for this, and now I could lay my whole self upon the altar in union with God's will.

On that high mountain, he who years ago in 1924 had called me to offer him a stammering tongue and to preach glad tidings to everyone to whom he sent me in the British Isles, and then in Palestine, and had called me to be one of his chauffeurs, and then to be a housekeeper for him in the Jerusalem Mission Hospital, now had a new purpose and call. For he said:

"Now you are to write it all down, Hannah. From now on you are to be both preacher and writer. Receive the pattern from me and write what I tell you, and inspire others by so doing."

It was all so still, unemotional, awed, and simple. One does not say at such a time as that, "But, Lord, I can't! I am deluding myself. I'm a crank, a monomaniac. My writing is feeble and ungrammatical and without form and voice, and ever so much of the spelling has to be corrected!"

No, the awe and the deep silence, simple submission and glad gratitude were all that I was conscious of, and a trust that he who called me to this task would give the "gift of creative writing" and enable me to pass on messages from him. I was to be made "bread" for others to feed upon: "Then flew one of the seraphims unto me, having a live coal in his hand . . . from off the altar" (Isa. 6:6), not this time to touch my lips (v. 7), but to touch my head and my hands and empower me to use a pen and to type whatever the Lord would give me to share in writing.

I knew, certainly and surely, that there, on the shoulder of the Echstock, with the beautiful wall of the mountain peaks all around, he had called me to write for him and had ordained me to use a gift which I had always wanted to receive. It had had to lie in abeyance until now, while I learned to use a stammering tongue in his service instead.

Two hours later I again entered the chairs of the Sesselbahn to go down the mountain. Down and down they ran and I sat and looked at the Ortstock and the Hoher Turm, and loved them almost as though they were fellow human beings, because they continually uttered forth God's praise and had been his messengers to me.

Gradually the whole circle of mountains seemed to rise higher and higher as the chairs ran lower and lower until once more they towered above me. We came to the precipice and the chair seats faced it, and for a few moments the sun was blotted out. Then came the woods and the green fields. I longed for the chairs to run on and on, bearing me up like a bird between earth and heaven. But the line dipped, and with a jerky rush we ran into the station and touched the ground again.

I walked slowly back to the Bergfrieden Haus, my whole being filled with the knowledge that I had been in God's presence, that I had heard his voice and knew his will. I had been carried up to the high places in one of his promises and brought safely down again. That thought was wonderfully comforting. He will not let me be lifted up in pride. He will give his "handmaiden" lowliness of heart and cause her to "abide under the shadow of his wing."

Cloud and Mist

BRAUNWALD MAY 31, 1949

This is my forty-fourth birthday and the last whole day in Braunwald. There is a thick curtain of mist, the thickest so far, and no sign that it will disperse. Everything is blotted out save the flowers just underneath my window and the tiny fir tree beside the path. Once again it is exactly as though the mountain ranges, the snow peaks, the green valley far below, and all the fields of flowers do not exist anywhere. If a person had never been here before, that one would not even dimly guess at what lies beyond the curtain of mist. All that I have looked upon and loved and rejoiced over has disappeared completely.

"But it is all there," says the loving Lord, "though you cannot see any of it, for it has been completely blotted out and apparently vanished into nothingness. But, remember, nothing is missing. It is invisible now but it is waiting to become visible again. And its last message to you is this: Believe steadfastly in the invisible things. 'For the things which are seen are temporal; but the things which are not seen are eternal'" (2 Cor. 4:18).

I went down to breakfast with my heart singing. I am to be carried up in the Sesselbahn of God's promise to the fulfillment of his purposes and plan. O my Lord! Enable me to prepare myself with joy, to put on my "Beautiful garments" (Isa. 52:1), and to go forth to meet God's will with joyful anticipation.

The fog outside matters nothing. It is my last day here and I am unable to go to the prayer place on the mountain slope. But that does not matter either. I ask for nothing better than to spend this last prayer morning—my birthday morning—in this room with you, Lord. Let the mist shut us in together. I have listened to the lovely voices of the mountains and the waterfalls and the fields and flowers. Now let me hear your voice and nothing else. The vanished beauties outside matter nothing.

"Let me see your face, Lord, and lay my hand in yours." And into my heart come singing words from the lovely Song of Songs. "The voice of my beloved! behold, he cometh leaping upon the mountains, skipping upon the hills" (Song of Sol. 2:8).

JUNE 1, 1949

From morning until night yesterday that thick curtain of mist shrouded everything. It never lifted for a moment. And now this morning I wake and find it still here. In two hours I must leave this blessed and beloved spot where I have learned so much. The last I saw of the mountains, which have become my friends, was on Sunday when they all stood majestically under a sky covered with black clouds tossed by a Fohn wind. That night the mist fell; the rain began and has lashed down ever since.

With one exception. On Monday afternoon the mist lifted slightly and I walked to Ohrenplatte, a famous view place. As the mist cleared occasionally in tiny patches, a dazzlingly white mountain would gleam through for a moment as though seen through a window. Once I stood holding my breath as the Scheidstockli peak suddenly shone out like a dazzling silver-white tower. A few minutes afterward when the mist had again covered it, another window suddenly opened and there was the Mattenstock, "high and lifted up"; and the sun which was invisible where I was shone on it so brilliantly that it looked as though a window in heaven (Mal. 3:10) had opened and we were looking through it at one of the "many mansions" (John 14:2), or a palace in the heavenly world. The mist made these isolated peaks look far higher than usual and quite unearthly, as though they really did belong to another world in the sky.

So as I walked along I kept thinking: It is only "the veil of sense which hangs dark between thy radiant face and mine," as the hymn so beautifully expresses it. Yes, it was as though the Lord drew aside little bits of the veil, here and there, so that I could look through to that radiant place on the other side of the curtain.

On a clear day I have no doubt that the view from Ohrenplatte is very lovely. A funny little aerial cable car runs up to it from the valley far below—a closed tram looking like a plump little airplane body without wings, according to the postcard pictures of it. Not like the open chairs of the Sesselbahn line. That afternoon when I visited it there was no view to be seen because of the mist, and I think it was almost lovelier, for those unexpected, fascinating glimpses of the peaks showing through the windows in the clouds were so breathtakingly beautiful.

I followed the narrow path along the mountainside; not up nor down, but around it, and oh! The flowers were so beautiful, close beside the path. The last field was almost filled with wild pansies smelling exquisitely sweet and fragrant.

When I got to the view place, there was of course no view. Only a café house loomed through the mist and a notice on the fence which said, "There is no other way to the view place except through here!" So I turned around and hurried home, rejoicing in the flowers and the scents and the mist, and with the words singing in my ears: Believe steadfastly in the invisible. Hold on to what God has shown you, though it appears to have no substance at all. "Faithful is he that calleth you, who also will do it" (1 Thess. 5:24).

When I left Braunwald in the mist and went down in the funicular railway to the valley far below and back to the roads and automobiles of all kinds (none of which can make the ascent to the heights of Braunwald), I received a last message through the flowers. There they were, in the mist, wet and lovely and ever so abundant. The tall, spiked purple and blue ones in thick clumps of rich color, and the carpets of little ones spread over the slopes, reminded me of the meadows I had seen above when the sun shone and gilded the golden kingcups and the gentians. And I thought of the narcissus fields toward which I was traveling, whose beauty had lingered in my memory for twenty-seven years, since the time when I went there with my mother for the last holiday she spent on earth.

Then it shone into my understanding that the message of the flowers was not just a reminder of God's loving-kindnesses and tender mercies in our own daily lives. But just like all the beauties of nature which have been uttering forth his messages to me and telling me what God wants us to understand through them, so the flowers speak of the beautiful loving-kindnesses and tender mercies which he wants to shower on others *through us*. Just as the Brumbach falls remind me of his love pouring through us to others, and the peaks speak of the high places of faith to which he wants to lead us in order that we may pour ourselves down with life-bringing joy to others, so our daily walk is to be like flower-filled fields offering beauty, comfort, cheer, and encouragement to everyone around about us.

Yes, indeed, this visit to beautiful Switzerland was not just for my own delight and pleasure, but so that I might have the privilege of sharing it in some God-given way with others. Who knows, perhaps even these little daily quiet-time notes may, sometime or other, be used by him for that lovely purpose also.

Visit to Les Avants

For nine hours I traveled from one end of Switzerland to the other, and at 3:30 p.m. reached Lausanne on the Lake of Geneva. Then the journey continued on up the mountains to Les Avants. But even here so far away from the Glarus mountains, the peaks were

also hidden in mist. Finally, at 5:10 p.m., the funicular rail landed me at the Hotel Saloup.

It is a very lovely hotel and I have a delightful room overlooking the lake. Already, after unpacking on this first evening, I have gone for a walk.

Now I make a confession. My feeling as I walked back to the hotel was one of real disappointment, even though it is very beautiful here and only the mountains are mist-shrouded.

Of course I am very tired, and I miss my dear, familiar mountain friends who taught me so much during the two weeks at Braunwald. But that is not what causes the disappointment; and it is not that the narcissus have gone by, for they are perfect and make the mountain slopes shine white as though they are covered with hoarfrost. But it is all so steep; either up or down and, apparently, no pleasant level paths along the sides of the slopes. And, worse still, all the narcissus fields appear to be out of reach. They are wired off with fences placarded with big notices which say: "It is forbidden to enter the narcissus fields beside the road without permission from the owners."

This I had *not* expected! Twenty-seven years ago my mother and our friends wandered freely wherever we chose. But now it all seems commercialized. Of course it is a famous and much-advertised beauty spot, especially at this time of year when the narcissus fields are in full bloom, and I suppose they must be preserved or the flowers would all be picked and carried off and sold by others. But it *is* a blow! Where am I to go apart to meet the Lord? Did I come to Les Avants to be faced with such a disappointment as this on my way back to all the unrest and threatening war in the Middle East?

I did pick a tiny handful of narcissus flowers which were blooming just outside the wire fence. And I saw the fields of them shining white in the evening light. But, yes, I was homesick for Braunwald!

And now this morning there is a steady mist and rain and I have only four days to spend here before I must leave and continue on my journey.

Evidently my Lord has something very important to teach me. And, oh! I do want to learn it. One thing I can do radiantly and gladly is: to go through each day praising for everything that happens. For the disappointments as well as the joys. For disappointments accepted with praise always seem to turn into extra-radiant blessings!

One verse keeps echoing in my mind and heart in connection

with these fenced-off narcissus fields, which I have traveled so far to see, hoping for the joy of sitting among them again and listening to my Lord and finding that I cannot reach them even if the sun comes out!

What a contrast between the free, lovely fields of Braunwald and the wired-off narcissus fields of Les Avants. But very tenderly and gently the Lord keeps reminding me of the verse in the Song of Songs: "A garden inclosed is my sister, my spouse; a spring shut up, a fountain sealed" (Song of Sol. 4:12).

Isn't that just what my life has been like, until my beloved Lord began breaking down the fences piece by piece? "A show garden," shut up and closed to so many ordinary people in whom I have felt no interest. Now my heart is to be made like open fields of flowers for the joy of others. As it is written in the same lovely song: "Awake, O north wind; and come, thou south; blow upon my garden, that the spices thereof may flow out. Let my beloved come into his garden, and eat his pleasant fruits.

"I am come into my garden, my sister, my spouse: I have gathered my myrrh with my spice . . . eat, O friends; drink, yea, drink abundantly" (4:16; 5:1).

Mont Blanc and the Way into the Narcissus Fields

By 5:00 p.m. on the first day the mist began to lift and there, spread out below, was the Lake of Geneva, shining like burnished brass as it reflected the evening sun, which I still could not see. For two hours I sat by the window watching it clear. The lake became a picture of radiant peace and joy, while the clouds slowly lifted and rolled away. At seven o'clock the crown of the day came. For at last there was clear blue sky and sunshine. When I went out on the terrace I looked up and saw all that I had traveled so far to see! There were the mountains I had known and loved as a little girl of four and six and eight years old when I had visited Switzerland with my parents. The Dent du Midi and Mont Blanc itself were now absolutely clear and free from cloud—radiant and glorious beyond words.

Later on I leaned out of one of the upper windows with two of the chambermaids. They said the mountains looked more beautiful than usual, because after the heavy rain the bright evening sunset poured over everything and a peculiar, almost unearthly beauty gilded all the colors in a way one sees only after heavy rain. There

was a golden radiance on the woods of dark fir trees, on the vivid green slopes, and on the fields of narcissus.

Towering heavenward, the tooth-edged summit of Dent du Midi turned gold in the sunset, with one narrow bar across the serene, shining peaks. "High and lifted up"—triumphant. The deep, snowy shoulders of Mont Blanc, the highest mountain in Switzerland, appeared behind it. All that I had wanted to see and feared would not become visible shone before me after all! And the high, serene, majestic peaks seemed to call across the burnished lake and say, "The God of peace fill you with all joy and peace in believing." And "make you perfect in every good work to do his will, working in you that which is wellpleasing in his sight, through Jesus Christ; to whom be glory forever and ever. Amen" (Heb. 13:21).

Next day the Lord led me to the perfect prayer place. Not among the steep, wired-off narcissus fields, but through the woods near the hotel and out into an open space.

Everything is here. The woods behind me; free, unwired slopes of narcissus flowers around and in front of me, and rising straight ahead, the Mountains of Savoic with the Dent du Midi in the foreground and lovely white Mont Blanc just behind. There is blue sky and brilliant sunshine and all is unspeakably lovely. Mist is rising from the valley and streaming up those mountain sides, but the peaks are clear. The sound of clanging cowbells rises from the valley beneath, and scarcely any other sound is to be heard.

I think I have come to understand the lesson which the Lord brought me back to Switzerland to learn in a special way. It concerns the great readjustment which I hope and believe is being made in me as he helps me to understand at last the reason why we are born into this fallen world and are entrusted with earthly mortal life. It is that we may learn, in a way which perhaps we could not do in heaven, how to abandon ourselves to loving God, who imagines and creates only the highest possible goodness.

In heaven everyone and everything is lovable, but as the Lord Jesus said, "If ye love them which love you, what reward have ye?" (Matt. 5:46). In heaven everyone loves everyone else, and in hell no one loves anyone. But on earth we are in a perfect environment for learning how to love as God loves: to abandon ourselves to loving the apparently unlovely people who remind us that in many ways we are still very unlovely ourselves!

Love is not a feeling. It is an overmastering passion to help and bless and deliver and comfort and strengthen and give joy to others just as the Lord Jesus always did.

Here on earth we have the opportunity to do what the God of love does all the time, and to learn to abandon ourselves to loving, to giving, to seeking, and to saving others. Not a lovely feeling of affection, or physical pleasure and satisfaction, but the extreme eternal ecstasy of creating happiness and good and blessed things for others to enjoy. To cast ourselves down like the Brumbach falls, in happy giving, asking for nothing in return except the joy of so doing. When we really begin to learn and practice that lesson we shall begin to feel "at home" in the eternal world of selfless love.

Here in Les Avants, God has been saying to me over and over again, "It is so happy to love without asking to be loved in return. Dare to be happy!"

It is not some feeling one waits for, nor some special person to evoke the love. It is an attitude of *will*. I will cast myself down in giving. The lower I go the more love I am able to transmit from God to others, just like the Lord of love himself, who was not content until he found and took the lowest place in the universe.

I spend my days on earth to learn this lesson, so that I may be able to love forever.

The Message of the Narcissus

Now too I have learned the lesson the narcissus were meant to teach me. Yesterday afternoon as I went for a walk, at first the path went down through a steep, slippery wood and then led me out onto far-stretching slopes covered with wild narcissus plants. There was nothing wired off there; and there were the flowers in all their fragrant glory. Multitudes and multitudes of them "which no man could number"—white slopes with here and there, buttercups shining like gold among the white-robed throngs, a mirror of those described in Revelation (Rev. 7:9-10).

The narcissus spoke their message to me quite clearly and, oh, so sweetly. It was not a message that I had expected to hear from them, but it was very, very beautiful. For as I stood on one of the slopes among them, almost unable to believe the beauty and to realize that all the slopes for miles around were covered in the same way, I made a discovery. I saw that all the multitudes of narcissus, without exception, faced down the hill! They all turned to look toward the valleys far below. When one stands among them and looks down the slope, one sees only their shining white backs. But

when one turns around and looks up the slope, one sees a multitude of little faces, each with a gold crown at the heart.

Yes, it really seemed as though I was seeing a reflection of what the Apostle John saw and described in Revelation:

> *I beheld, and, lo, a great multitude, which no man could number . . . stood before the throne, and before the Lamb, clothed with white robes, and palms in their hands; and cried with a loud voice, saying, Salvation to our God which sitteth upon the throne, and unto the Lamb. . . . And one of the elders answered, saying unto me, What are these which are arrayed in white robes? and whence came they? And I said unto him, Sir, thou knowest. And he said to me, These are they which came out of great tribulation, and have washed their robes, and made them white in the blood of the Lamb. Therefore are they before the throne of God, and serve him day and night in his temple: and he that sitteth on the throne shall dwell among them. They shall hunger no more, neither thirst any more; neither shall the sun light on them, nor any heat. For the Lamb which is in the midst of the throne shall feed them, and shall lead them unto living fountains of waters: and God shall wipe away all tears from their eyes (7:9-10, 13-17).*

Yes, that is what the narcissus said as they stood there, tier upon tier and row upon row, all over the mountain slopes, and all of them looking eagerly down, as from an amphitheater, to the valley below. They spoke to me of all those who have learned the lesson of eternal love, and have passed on before us through the veil of sense, into the realm of holy love in the light of God's presence. There they are, watching eagerly to see how we learn the same lesson. My own father and mother are among them. If they could call to me from the world into which they have passed, I feel sure this is what they would both say: "Hannah, it is happy to love. Abandon yourself to loving. Drink of the Spirit of the Lord of love and cast self down. It is the Cross. But it is Life and eternal joy."

After that I went far down into the valley and then began to rise on the other side of it. Passing through a wood, I came to a spot of wild rock garden, down which a little waterfall poured itself from pool to pool. In the pool nearest to the bridge on which I paused to rest, there were seven unhappy looking little sticks going around and around endlessly in a kind of miniature whirlpool. I leaned on the side of the bridge watching them, waiting to see them escape from the eddies and go over the lip of the pool with the rejoicing water as it leaped down to lower and lower places. But presently I realized that the poor, miserable things would never take the plunge, but would go on whirling around dizzily, quite unable to get free, plunge over the edge, and find freedom far below.

I turned away at last, left them, and went up the hill, thinking of the Brumbach falls and the song which all free waters sing all over the world, "Come let us go the lowly way. Lower, lower every day."

For an hour I went higher and higher up the hill, always surrounded by narcissus. I never saw such a sight before. There were no other hotels in the valley except the one where I was staying, and there were only a few apparently empty chalets. So I walked among the narcissus for one hour as though I really was blessed to be among the white-robed throng who have been made perfect in love, beholding their joy and dazzled by their glory.

"These are they that have come out of great tribulation," from the earthly world into the heavenly one. They have washed their robes and made them white in the blood of the Lamb, being made conformable unto his death.

The Geneva Fountain

The day to leave Switzerland came, and I had come down from the high places of the mountains and had to wait a few hours in Geneva. I sat in the Public Gardens beside the lake and looked at the famous Geneva fountain, the symbol of the League of Nations.

At first sight it is wonderfully impressive and spectacular, and the water leaps up to an amazing height and then descends in far-flung spray. But the longer I looked at it, it seemed, somehow, to become strangely unsatisfying. Then, in memory, I stood again beside the precipice at Braunwald and saw the waters leaping over the edge in abandoned giving. And I learned a new lesson.

For the Geneva fountain is exactly the opposite of the Brumbach waterfall. The fountain is manmade and strangely useless and artificial. It is like a symbol of unreal, forced love, just as the waterfall on the mountain slopes is the symbol of true love, freely pouring itself down in an ecstasy of giving. The Geneva fountain is forced up and falls down at once to the place from which it was

driven upward. As soon as it is no longer forced against its natural inclination, it collapses. Then the same water is used over and over again, performing no useful function except to appear attractive and suggest a delight which is not real and spontaneous—whereas the real waterfall in the mountains is always exultantly giving itself and losing itself and carrying life wherever it goes.

O my Lord, I beg you to make that the wondrous, joyful ideal of my life here on earth, day after day.

The Highest Place of All

The Swiss airplane on which I was to fly back to Israel took off at 3:00 p.m. in perfect weather. The mist and rain were over and gone. The land, as I left it, was bathed in sunshine and the sky a vivid, heavenly blue. And my Lord had one last glorious thing to show me.

We flew over the Alps for more than an hour. I had not expected that, and could never have imagined what it would mean. Had we left a day earlier, it would all have been invisible and shrouded in rain and mist. But as it was, it became to me almost what John saw on Patmos.

The Lake of Geneva was left behind and far below us, and then we flew past Mont Blanc, the highest mountain in Switzerland. It towered up like a great and glorious white throne, "high and lifted up" above all the other peaks. All the Swiss Alps, row on row and tier on tier of endless snow peaks, formed a vast semicircle, like the thrones of the elders around it. For almost an hour that great towering throne remained in sight as other mountain ranges in nearby countries took the place of the Swiss ones. The boundless sapphire sky overhead seemed just as the hymn describes it.

Angels and archangels must have gathered there;
Cherubim and Seraphim thronged the air.

It seemed to me that I saw there, in symbolic form, the source of true love; the great and everlasting height from whence, in the presence of angels and archangels, "and all the company of heaven," the true Eternal Falls of love flow down from the heights in an ecstasy of self-giving. Actually, a part of God's love continually leaves the throne for the mist-shrouded earthy valleys below—just as the Lord Jesus Christ came down to earth as the "Water of Life" to the low places far beneath. It is written:

> *Let this mind be in you, which was also in Christ Jesus: who, being in the form of God, thought it not robbery to be equal with God: but made himself of no reputation, and took upon him the form of a servant, and was made in the likeness of men: and being found in fashion as a man, he humbled himself, and became obedient unto death, even the death of the cross. Wherefore God also hath highly exalted him, and given him a name which is above every name: that at the name of Jesus every knee should bow, of things in heaven, and things in earth, and things under the earth; and that every tongue should confess that Jesus Christ is Lord, to the glory of God the Father. . . . That ye may be blameless and harmless, the sons of God, without rebuke, in the midst of a crooked and perverse nation, among whom ye shine as lights in the world; holding forth the word of life (Phil. 2:5-11, 15-16).*

Yes, from the highest place in the universe, the divine Love leaped down to the lowest place of all. The little Brumbach falls of the world are only tiny pictures and images through which the Creator teaches us this staggering truth. And Mont Blanc and the Alps are just a shadowy picture also of the nature of eternal love. Oh! blest be the Creator, because he himself shows us this awesome and glorious truth through them: For he also longs to make us little true images and reflectors of his divine love.

In that hour, in the airplane above the Alps, my little narrow, cold, self-centered human heart caught a tiny but staggering glimpse of what it means to be the sons and daughters of the eternal God of love. We are called to love with the fullest capacity of which we are capable. To love as he loves, and so to be an echo—faint and feeble, but a true one—of that eternal self, giving us drops of the water of life, poured out in the cataract of that divine self-giving.

Then the voice of our Father said with tender, gentle love, "Hannah, let me help you to practice the lessons which you have been learning. Talk about them and demonstrate them back there in the sorrowful Holy Land to which you are returning. Claim the great and precious promises which I have given you, so that you may become more and more a partaker of my divine nature of perfect, holy, selfless, divine love."

So the flight continued on over the lands and countries beneath, and then over the Mediterranean Sea, until we reached the shores of the Holy Land and came down at the Lydda Airport. There I found myself entering upon a completely new life of unexpected surprises and challenges. I began my writing ministry, and then very soon, started traveling from country to country around the world.

Six years later, in 1955, I was privileged just once more to visit Braunwald, and there, sitting on the green slopes overlooking the Ortstock mountain, I wrote *Hinds' Feet on High Places*, and so brought to birth in written form the messages conceived in that same place six years earlier.

Oh, what a life of wonderful joy, adventure, and ever-deepening love the Good Shepherd leads us all to! As we follow him along the path of life, let us leave him to choose every step of the way, as we live in his radiant presence and are ever led to still higher places.

Glory be to him forever! Amen.

Hannah Hurnard

A Brief Autobiography

I WAS BROUGHT UP IN AN evangelical home and environment where religious beliefs were considered far and away the most important things in the world. In comparison with them nothing else really mattered, and worldliness and anything that tended to make the spiritual life and growth of the soul seem unimportant were inexorably excluded. Spiritual things and religious doctrines were obviously of such vital value to my parents that I could not fail to be impressed with a deep sense of their importance.

One could not live in my home and be carelessly indifferent to the possibility of the existence of a spiritual world. I could not fail to realize that "to love the Lord their God with all their heart and their soul and their strength" was the steady aim of my parents' life, that all their joy and satisfaction was found in seeking to serve him, and that they held everything they possessed as a trust from him. My father's whole life seemed to be summed up in the words, "It is required in stewards that a man be found faithful." As for my mother, through all the years of her ill-health, suffering, and almost constant pain, she was so joyful a lover of the Lord Jesus that when she spoke his name her very voice changed and her face became lighted as though an inner lamp shone through the earthly vessel. "His name is as ointment poured forth, therefore do we love him," is the verse which I most closely associate with her memory.

As a child of eleven, I did, as I hoped and believed, become

"converted" by offering myself to the unseen Savior whose existence I did not at that time doubt.

But the outward expression of spiritual worship in which I was brought up seemed to me, from my earliest years, dreary and depressing, and though, as a child, I felt that religion must certainly be the most important thing in the world, I simply could not find any reality or satisfaction in it. I dreaded the type of service we were obliged to attend, and Sunday was a nightmare hanging over me the whole week.

I prayed, but there was no answer. I went to gospel services, and was unutterably bored and depressed. I repented, but I couldn't stop doing wrong things. I read the Bible and found it the dullest and most lifeless book in the world. It conveyed absolutely nothing to my longing soul, although it was held up as the infallible Word of God, the one channel through which he chose to reveal himself. Nothing helped. The saving power never came. The means of grace didn't work. I simply couldn't believe.

By the time I had reached the middle teens I could no longer believe in the existence of God, for there seemed absolutely no way of getting in touch with him.

I was a miserable, morbid, self-centered person who never felt love for anyone, shut up to my own torment. Till I was nineteen I never remember feeling happy, though of course I sometimes stopped feeling unhappy. I had two hateful and tormenting handicaps. One, a horrible stammer, which whenever I tried to speak, kept me mouthing in a desperate effort to get the words out. Until I was nineteen, I never went into a shop alone, nor onto a bus or train, or anywhere where I would be obliged to speak. As a child, when we were playing in the garden alone and I was natural and unselfconscious, I could often say whole sentences, but if spoken to or asked a question, the ghastly struggles began at once.

I simply hated people, the unfeeling ones, and even the kind ones who looked away and were horribly sorry and embarrassed. At school I suffered torments and appeared a perfect fool, always saying I didn't know the answers to questions because I couldn't get the answers out.

The other handicap was, in some ways, even worse than the stammer. I was obsessed by tormenting fears, some quite ordinary ones such as many other people share, but also many abnormal ones, at least perhaps I experienced them to an abnormal degree and more or less continuously. I felt terror of the dark, terror of heights, a maddening terror of being shut in anywhere, terror of crowds, of being ill and of fainting and losing consciousness, and above all, a daily and nightly experienced horror of death.

The older I grew the more I felt the humiliation and hurt of my stammer. Morning after morning I awoke feeling that I simply could not face another day. I longed for the courage to commit suicide. Thus, I grew more and more morbid and tormented and shut up to myself, unable to think of anything but my own unspeakable wretchedness.

All this time, though I would have given anything to believe that there was a God who could help even me, he seemed to take no notice, to pay no attention to my despairing prayers and to become more and more unreal and inaccessible.

Why do I emphasize all of this? Because in one half hour, when I was nineteen years of age, my whole life was changed, and this hateful, abnormal husk split, and fell off, and left me, not with a new physical makeup or another mental outfit but with an absolutely transformed outlook.

This is how the amazing transformation took place. In 1924, my father, the only person on earth for whom I felt real affection, because he was my only refuge, and being a stammerer himself could understand my agony, told me that he wanted to take me to the convention at Keswick. I was horrified at the very thought of being obliged to go to religious meetings all day long, shut up with a crowd of people in a tent, and at first I refused. But finally we made a bargain together. I would go with him to the convention and would attend one meeting each morning and one meeting each evening, and the rest of the day I was to be free to wander about on the hills alone.

So I went through the whole week of the convention, attending two meetings a day, and it seemed that absolutely nothing spoke to me. God was as unreal at the end as at the beginning.

On Friday evening the convention ended, but on Saturday morning the great missionary meeting was held. Twelve men and women got up, one after another, and with radiant faces told us of God's transforming power which they themselves had actually seen operating in countless heathen lives.

I cannot remember a word any of them said. But what no text or passage from the Bible and no earnest speaker at the convention had been able to do, those twelve missionary men and women accomplished. It is, of course, truer to say, as I now realize, that they finished the work the rest of the convention had begun. They put the final touch. For as I sat there in utter wretchedness and looked at their radiant faces, and heard the certainty in their voices, my heart said despairingly, "It must be true. There must be a God after all who is able to save and transform even the most wretched and tormented; able and willing, apparently, to save everybody but me. Why can't I find him?"

When the twelve missionaries had finished, the chairman rose to his feet and asked if there were any young men and women in that great audience who had heard God calling them to the mission field. If they had responded in their hearts, would they stand up? There was a sound of rustling all over the great tent, as scores, perhaps hundreds, of young people rose to their feet. Then the chairman asked if there were any parents there who were ready to give their children to the mission field if God called them. My father rose in his place beside me, and stood with the hundreds of other parents.

That was the last straw. I struggled to my feet and hurried out of the tent. Getting on my bicycle, I tore back to our lodging house outside the town, rushed into my little room, and locking the door fell on my knees beside the bed. And at last in an extremity of despair and misery of heart I cried out aloud, "O God, if there is a God anywhere, you must make yourself real to me. If you exist and are really what these people describe you to be, you can't leave me like this."

I seized my Bible and held it closed in my hands, and cried again, "O God, if there is a God, your followers say that you speak to them through the Bible. If you are real, speak to me through this book too."

I flapped the Bible open and looked at it. It had opened at a chapter in 1 Kings.

So I began to read, and at the very first words on which my eyes lighted I felt a strange mental shock. For I had opened at 1 Kings 18 where Elijah challenged the Israelites to believe in the one true God, and declared that he would prove that he existed. And the verse where I began to read said, "How long halt ye between two opinions? If the Lord be God, follow him."

The thought came to me vividly and clearly, in a dreadful flash of mental enlightenment. "What this unknown God is going to demand before he makes himself real is that I yield to him my stammering tongue, and agree to be his witness and messenger."

All the time then this was why he had never made himself real. He was waiting until I would agree to give him my stammering tongue and tell him that he could use it in any way that he chose.

How he managed it I still cannot understand, but at last there came a moment when I cried out again, "O God, if there is a God, if you will make yourself real to me, I will yield my stammering mouth."

I went into that room at 1:00 p.m. on July 26, 1924, and I came out of it at 1:30 p.m. after that half hour of agony, completely transformed. Life was utterly different and radiant from that hour.

My fearful nature was still there. My stammer was still there. My dread of people was still there; and so was my complete ignorance of how to begin thinking about others and considering their interests. I was still the old Hannah, but in some miraculous and mysterious way I had been lifted into a completely new mental and spiritual environment, out of the borderland of outer darkness, into the light and glory of heaven.

Two and a half months passed, and in the autumn the time came for me to go to Ridgelands Bible College. I was still stammering, but not so badly as before, and I had even managed, after a great struggle, to pray very briefly in public.

I decided that I must go alone on the train and on the underground, though I had never done such a thing before, even though I was then nearly twenty years of age.

Obedience was always tested to the hilt. It never became easy, and the inner suggestion invariably presented itself, that one day

the power would fail and he would let me down. I learned that I must never pay any attention to these fears and doubts.

In one way I lived a double existence in those early years, for I was constantly attacked by the old fears and misgivings and wretched physical feelings, and nearly every day there were agonizing inner struggles before any act of obedience to some new call of his. And yet, on the other hand, every obedience was followed by a flood of amazing joy impossible to describe.

Thus I gradually came to realize that these two handicaps which had so tormented me were, in reality, two special love gifts from the Lord. They were the two sharp nails which nailed me to him, so that I could never want or dare to go on my own again.

When I had finished my two years at Ridgelands Bible College I joined The Friends Evangelistic Band for further training in work that would prepare me for the mission field. The Band was an interdenominational faith mission doing evangelistic work in the villages of England and Ireland.

The motto of the Band at that time was "Ready for Anything." Ready for anything the Lord asked us to attempt and ready to go anywhere he sent us. I was twenty-one when I joined them, and I rather embarrassed and shocked my relatives by traveling about the country in a caravan, holding open air meetings and missions in village after village.

After I had been working in the Evangelistic Band for four years, I was sent over to Ireland again to do deputation work, traveling over the country telling about the needs of the unevangelized villages of England and Ireland. One Saturday afternoon I was invited to go with a party of factory and shop girls on an outing to Ireland's Eye, one of the beauty spots near Dublin. After a time I wandered away alone and climbed to the highest rocky peak.

I had no idea that God was going to speak to me in a special way, or that I was to receive a clear call which once again would revolutionize my whole way of life. I still felt that eventually the Lord wanted me to become a missionary, but I had no idea where that would be.

Up there on Ireland's Eye, I had no special subject in mind, and began to read just where the Bible opened, which happened to be the ninth chapter of Daniel. As I slowly read through this wonderful prayer, pondering on it verse by verse, an unexpected and startling thing happened. A thought came into my mind, as though naturally following the train of previous thoughts, but with a clarity and significance which seemed a personal challenge.

"Hannah, would you be willing to identify yourself with the Jewish people in the same way, if I asked you to?" I found my thoughts answering him in great distress.

"But, Lord, I'm sorry to say I don't like the Jews a bit. They are the last people in the world I feel interested in trying to help. How could I be of any use as a missionary to the Jews if I don't like them?"

"If you will yield to me wholly and agree to go, I will make you able to love them and identify yourself with them. It all depends upon your will."

I scrambled to my feet and knelt down on the rock which had become an altar, for this was a definite offering of myself, an act of deep worship and glad surrender. It concluded a conversation and sealed my readiness to obey. I knelt then on the rocks and said, "Here I am, Lord. I will go as a missionary to thy people Israel."

When I came down from the rocky peak of Ireland's Eye, and began to tell my friends that God had called me to go to Palestine as a missionary, how little, how absurdly little there was to show for it. The friend with whom I was staying asked how I knew I had a call and how it came to me.

When I told the leader of the Band I felt that God was now calling me to the mission field, namely, to Palestine, he and others with him were at first very doubtful.

It was harder still when, after more prayer for guidance, I wrote to the secretary of the only interdenominational mission that I knew which was working in Palestine, and offered my services. Among the questions sent to me to answer was, naturally enough, one about special training and qualifications, and another asking why I felt called to Jewish work in Palestine, and there was nothing that I could explain except a "still small voice" speaking through my thoughts at Ireland's Eye, saying, "Will you go and identify yourself with my people Israel?"

I answered the questions to the best of my ability and in due course a letter came back saying they had noted that I had no special qualifications, as a trained nurse or teacher or secretary, all of which they were needing, but there was, at present, no opening for a lady evangelist. Among the Jews, I was told, women were not generally considered worth listening to if they tried to preach or teach men.

Every step of the way out to the mission field was tested. The doctor, as well as most of my friends, did not think that my health or nervous temperament fitted me to work abroad, and I could not but agree with them.

Beside that, I knew that as I had no practical training I could not expect a missionary society to employ me as a salaried missionary if they were not needing an evangelistic worker. But in the end it was agreed that I should go to Haifa on trial, paying my own expenses and undertaking to assist in any way in which I proved capable, being ready to act as a stopgap wherever required, until it would be seen what work the Lord really wanted me to do, or would open for me.

I crept meekly, and oh so thankfully, into Palestine on January 21, 1932.

How truly and joyfully I can testify as I look back over my path of life, "Faithful is he that calleth you, who also will do it."

Amen, Lord. Yes, ever since that radiant day when I knelt beside my bed at Keswick and thou didst take me to be thine own, thy grace has been sufficient for me, and thou hast enabled poor Miss Much-Afraid to keep following. No giant has been allowed to turn her back, no evil to come nigh her dwelling.

This autobiography has been abridged from *Hearing Heart*. A full account of Hannah Hurnard's ministry in Israel is given in *Wayfarer in the Land*.

Books by Hannah Hurnard

GOD'S TRANSMITTERS. Prayer need not be a burdensome duty. It is meant to be a joyful and creative privilege.

HEARING HEART. An intimate, autobiographical look into the life of author and missionary Hannah Hurnard.

HINDS' FEET ON HIGH PLACES. An allegory dramatizing the journey each of us must take before we can learn the secret of living life "in high places."

KINGDOM OF LOVE. The ABCs of love presented here will enable us to represent God's love to those around us.

MOUNTAINS OF SPICES. An allegory about human weaknesses and strengths, comparing the spices in Song of Solomon to the fruits of the Spirit.

WALKING AMONG THE UNSEEN. A call to practice the New Testament pattern as the normal standard of life.

WAYFARER IN THE LAND. An epic of the author's experiences in bringing the Wayfarer's message to remote settlements in Israel.

WINGED LIFE. This book presents five keys that will transform the way you think and make the "winged life" a reality.

I HAVE LOVED THEE WITH AN EVERLASTING LOVE: THEREFORE WITH LOVINGKINDNESS HAVE I DRAWN THEE.

JEREMIAH 31:3